THE MAN WHO LOVED
LEVITTOWN

THE MAN WHO LOVED
LEVITTOWN

W. D. WETHERELL

UNIVERSITY OF PITTSBURGH PRESS

1925

Published by the University of Pittsburgh Press, Pittsburgh, Pa., 15260
Copyright © 1985, W. D. Wetherell
All rights reserved
Feffer and Simons, Inc., London
Manufactured in the United States of America

Library of Congress Cataloging in Publication Data

Wetherell, W. D.
  The man who loved Levittown.

  Contents: The man who loved Levittown—Spitfire autumn—If a
woodchuck could chuck wood—[etc.]
  I. Title.
PS3573.E9248M3   1985   813'.54   85-1172
ISBN 0-8229-3520-1 (alk. paper)

"The Man Who Loved Levittown" originally appeared in *The Atlantic Monthly*, "If a
Woodchuck Could Chuck Wood" was first published in *Virginia Quarterly Review*, "The
Lob" is reprinted from *Colorado Quarterly*, "Nickel a Throw" was originally published in
New England Review and Bread Loaf Quarterly, "Narrative of the Whale Truck Essex" first
appeared in *The Michigan Quarterly Review*, "Volpi's Farewell" was first published in
Graffiti, and "Spitfire Autumn" is reprinted from *Virginia Quarterly Review*.

"The Bass, the River and Sheila Mant" won the 1983 PEN Syndicated Fiction Prize and
first appeared in the following newspapers: *Arizona Republic*, *Chicago Tribune*, *Hartford
Courant*, *Kansas City Star*, *Miami Herald*, *Newsday*, *Oregonian*, *Rocky Mountain News*, and
San Francisco Chronicle. "North of Peace" won the 1984 PEN Syndicated Fiction Prize
and first appeared in the following newspapers: *Hartford Courant*, *Miami Herald*, *San
Francisco Chronicle*, and *Village Advocate*.

For Katherine and David

C O N T E N T S

THE MAN WHO LOVED
LEVITTOWN

The Man Who Loved Levittown

YOU realize what I had to do to get this place? It was thirty-odd years ago come July. I'm just out of the Army. Two kids, twins on their way, a wife who's younger than I am, just as naive, just as crazy hopeful. We're living in the old neighborhood with my folks four to a room. All along I've got this idea. Airplanes. P-40s, these great big 20s. We're slogging through Saipan, they're flying over it. DiMaria, I tell myself, this war is going to end, when it does that's where you want to be, up there in the blue not down here in the brown. Ever since I'm a kid I'm good with machines, what I do is figure I'll get a job making them. Grumman. Republic. Airborne. They're all out there on Long Island. I tell Kathy to watch the kids, I'll be back tonight, wish me luck. I borrow the old man's Ford, out I go. Brooklyn Bridge, Jamaica Avenue, Southern State, and I'm there.

Potato fields. Nothing but. French-fried heaven, not another car in sight. I stop at a diner for coffee. Farmers inside look me over like I'm the tax man come to collect. Bitter. Talking about how they were being run off their places by these new housing developments you saw advertised in the paper, which made me mad because here I am a young guy just trying to get started, what were we supposed to do . . . live on East Thirteenth Street the rest of our lives? The being run off part was pure phooey anyhow, because they were making plenty on it, they never had it so good.

4   But hearing them talk made me curious enough to drive around a little exploring.

Sure enough, here's this farmhouse all boarded up. Out in front is an ancient Chevy piled to the gunwales with old spring beds, pots and pans. Dust Bowl, Okies, *Grapes of Wrath* . . . just like that. I drive up to ask directions half expecting Marjorie Main. Instead there's this old man climbing up to the top of the pile. He's having a hell of a time getting up there. Once he does he stands with his hand shielding his eyes looking around the horizon like someone saying good-bye.

Maybe I'm just imagining it now but it seems to me it was so flat and smooth those days even from where I stood on the ground I could see just as far as he could . . . see the entire Island, right across the entire thing. Out to Montauk with waves breaking atop the rocks so green and bright they made me squint. Back this way over acres of pine trees, maybe one, maybe two lonely railroad tracks, nothing else except lots of ospreys which were still around those days. Then he turns, I turn, we look over to where the Jones Beach water tower is jutting up like the Leaning Tower of Pisa. Just this side of it the Great South Bay is wall-to-wall scallops and clams. You look left up the other way toward the North Shore there's these old ivy-covered mansions being torn down, pieces of confetti, broken champagne bottles all over the lawn. I have to squint a little now . . . I can just make out the shore of the Sound with all these sandy beaches that had "No Trespassing" signs on them, only a man in a yellow vest is walking along now ripping them down . . . not two seconds later the beach is crowded with little kids splashing in the waves. Then after that we both look the other way back toward New York . . . the old man tottering up there in the breeze . . . over these abandoned hangars at Roosevelt Field where everybody took off to Europe alone from back in the twenties, then out toward where the skyscrapers are in the distance. I see the Empire State Building . . . for some crazy reason I wave. Then in a little closer over one or two small villages, acres of potato fields, and no matter which way you look . . . Sound side, Bay side, South Shore, North Shore . . . there's the sound of hammers, the smell of sawdust, little houses going up in clusters, carpenters working bare-chested in the sun. The old man is looking all this over, then looks right at me, you know what he says? "I hope it poisons you!" With that he fell off the bundle, his son had to prop him back up, they drove away in a cloud of dust.

Fine. I drive down the road a little farther, here are these new houses up close. Small ones. Lots of mud. Old potatoes sticking out of it like dried-up turds. Broken blocks off two-by-fours. Nails, bits of shingle. In front of each house or half house or quarter house is a little lawn. Fuzzy green grass. Baby grass. At every corner is an empty post waiting for a street name to be fitted in the slot on top. A man comes along in a jeep, shuffles through the signs, scratches his head, sticks in one says LINDBERGH, drives off. Down the street is a Quonset hut with a long line of men waiting out in front, half of them still in uniform. Waiting for jobs I figure, like in the Depression . . . here we go again. But here's what happens. A truck comes along, stops in front of the house, half a dozen men pile out . . . in fifteen minutes they've put in a bathroom. Pop! Off they go to the next house, just in time, too, because here comes another truck with the kitchen. Pop! In goes the kitchen. They move on one house, here comes the electricians. Pop! Pop! Pop! the house goes up.

There's no one around except this guy in overalls planting sticks in the little brown patches stamped out of the grass. "My name's DiMaria," I tell him. "What's yours?" "Bill Levitt," he says. "And what's the name of this place anyhow?" "Levittown." And then it finally dawns on me. What these men are lined up for isn't work, it's homes!

"How much does one of these babies cost?" I ask him casually.

6   He picks at his nose, leans his shovel against the tree. "Seven thousand," he says, looking right at me. "One hundréd dollars down." "Oh yeah?" I say, still casual. But I kind of half turn, take out my wallet, take a peek inside. "I only have eighty-three." He looks me over. "You a veteran?" "You bet. Four year's worth, I don't miss it at all either." He calls over to a man helping with the sinks. "Hey, Johnson!" he yells. "Take this guy's money and let him pick out whichever one he wants. Mr. DiMaria," he says, shaking my hand. "You've just bought yourself a house."

I will never until the day I die forget the expression on Kathy's face when I got back that night. Not only have I bought a house but that same afternoon Grumman hires me at three bucks an hour plus overtime. "Honey, " I said, "get your things together, let's go, hubba, hubba, we're on our way home!"

I'm not saying it wasn't tough those first years. It was plenty tough. I worked to six most nights, sometimes seven. When I got home I fixed hamburgers for the kids since Kathy was out working herself. Minute she gets home, out I go pumping gas on the turnpike for mortgage money. Ten years we did that. But what made it seem easier was that everyone else on Lindbergh was more or less in the same boat. Young GIs from old parts of the city somewhere working at the big plants farther out. There were some pretty good men on that block. Scotty. Mike. Hank Zimmer. There wasn't anything we couldn't build or fix between us. I once figured out just among the guys on Lindbergh, let alone Hillcrest, we had enough talent to make ourselves an F-14. You know how complicated an F-14 is? Cabin cruisers, porches, garages . . . you name it, we built it. That's why this little boxes stuff was pure phooey. Sure they were little boxes when we first started. But what did we do? The minute we got our mitts on them we started remodeling them, adding stuff, changing them around.

There wasn't anything we wouldn't do for each other. Babysit,

drive someone somewhere, maybe help out with a mortgage pay-
ment someone couldn't meet. You talk about Little League. Me
and Mike are the ones *invented* it. We got the field for it, organized
teams, umpired, managed, coached. Both my boys played; we
once had a team to the national finals, we would have won if
O'Brien's kid hadn't booted a grounder. But it was nice on summer nights to see dads knocking out flies to their kids, hearing the
ball plop into gloves, see the wives sitting there on the lawns
talking, maybe watering the lawn. The swimming pool up the
block, the shops, the schools. It was nice all those things. People
take them for granted nowadays, they had to start somewhere,
right?

I'll never forget those years. The fifties. The early sixties. We
were all going the same direction . . . thanks to Big Bill Levitt we
all had a chance. You talk about dreams. Hell, we had ours. We had
ours like nobody before or since ever had theirs. SEVEN THOU-
SAND BUCKS! ONE HUNDRED DOLLARS DOWN! We were
cowboys out there. We were the pioneers.

I'll be damned if I know where the end came from. It was a little
after the time I finished putting the sun roof over the porch. Kathy
was in the living room yelling, trying to get my attention.
"Tommy, come over here quick! Look out the window on Scotty's
front lawn!" There planted right smack in the middle is a sign.
FOR SALE! You know what my first reaction was? I was scared.
Honest to God. I can't tell you why, but seeing that sign scared
me. It scared me so much I ran into the bathroom, felt like being
sick. Steady, DiMaria, I said. It's a joke like the time he put floun-
ders under the hubcaps. Ginger needed a walk anyway, I snap a
collar on her, out we go.

"So, Scotty, you kidding or what?" I say. Scotty just smiles.
"We're pulling up, moving to Florida." "You mean you're taking a
vacation down there? Whereabouts, Vero Beach?" He shakes his

8 head. "Nope, Tommy. For good. I'm retiring. Twenty-five years of this is enough for anyone. The kids are on their own now. The house is too big for just the two of us. Carol and I are heading south. Thirty-nine thousand we're asking. Thirty-nine thousand! Whoever thought when we bought these shacks they would someday go for that?"

The twenty-five years part stunned me because it was like we'd all started yesterday as far as I was concerned. But the Florida part, that really killed me. Florida was someplace you got oranges from, where the Yanks spent March. But to actually move there?

"Come on, Scotty," I laugh. "You're kidding me, right?" "Nope. This guy is coming to look at the house this afternoon."

A guy named Mapes bought Scotty's place. A young kid worked for the county. I went over and introduced myself. "I've been here twenty-nine years," I said. "I knew Bill Levitt personally." "Who?" he asks. "Big Bill Levitt, the guy this town is named after." "Oh," he says, looking stupid. "I always thought that was an Indian name."

I should have known right there. But being the idiot I am, I take him out behind the house, show him the electricity meter. "Tell you a little secret," I whisper. "Got a screwdriver?"

I'd been helping myself to some surplus voltage ever since I got out there. Everyone on Lindbergh did. We were all practically engineers; when we moved in we couldn't believe it, all this electricity up there, all those phone lines going to waste. It was the land of milk and honey as far as we were concerned; all we had to do was plug in and help ourselves. I'm telling Mapes this but he's standing there looking dubious. "Uh, you sure this is okay?" "You kidding? There's plenty more where that came from. They'll never miss it. Twist that, jig this, weld that there, you're in business." "Oh yeah," he says, but you can tell he doesn't get it because when I hand him the screwdriver he drops it. "Oops!" he giggles.

Meantime his bride comes along. Beads. Sandals. No, repeat, NO
bra. "Jennifer," he says, "this is Mr. DiMaria from next door."
"Call me Tommy, how are you?" The first words out of her
mouth, you know what they are? "How many live in your
house?" "Uh, two. My wife, myself." She looks me over, puffs on
something I don't swear was a Winston. "That's not many for a
whole house. If you ever decide to sell my kid sister's getting
married. They need a place bad. Let me know next week, will
yah?"

That was Mapes. Silver, the sheepherder took over O'Brien's,
was even worse. "Hello, welcome to the neighborhood," I said
walking across his lawn, my hand out. "That your dog?" he asks,
pointing toward Ginger rolling in the pachysandra. "Yeah. Come
here, Ginger. Shake the man's hand." "Dogs are supposed to be
leashed, mister. If you don't get him off my property in five minutes, I'm calling the pound and having the animal destroyed."
With that he walks away.

Welcome to Lindbergh Street.

I'm not saying it was because of that but right about then a lot of
old-timers put their houses on the market. It was sad because
before, guys like Scotty could at least say they wanted to go to
Florida, actually look forward to it. But now? Now the ones who
ran out ran out because they were forced to. Taxes up, cost of
living, heating oil, you name it. Here we'd had these homes for
thirty years, broke our backs paying the mortgages off, you'd
think it'd become easier for us now. Forget it. It was *harder*. It was
harder keeping them than getting them.

What made it worse was the price everyone was getting. Forty
thousand. Fifty thousand. The ones who stayed couldn't handle it
anymore thinking they'd only paid seven. The real estate bastards
dazzled them into selling even though they didn't want to. That
was the sad part of it, seeing them try to convince themselves

10   Florida would be nice. "We're getting a condominium," they'd say, the same somebody told you they were getting a valve bypass or a hysterectomy. "Well, I kind of like fishing," Mike said when he broke the news to me. "Don't they have good fishing down there?" "Sure they have good fishing, Mike," I told him. "Good fishing if you don't mind having your finger sucked by a water moccasin."

You think I'm exaggerating? You expect me to maybe say something good about the place? What if all your friends were taken away from you by coronaries, you wouldn't be too fond of heart disease, right? That's exactly the way I look at Florida. Guys like Buzz and Scotty think they're going to find Paradise down there, they're going to find mosquitoes, snakes, walking catfish, old people, that's it. This guy I know in the plant had his vacation down there. He thought it would be nice, no crime, no muggers. The first night there a Cuban breaks into his trailer, ties him up, rapes his wife, takes everything they had. Florida? You guys can have it. If Ponce de Leon were alive today he'd be living in Levittown.

But anyhow, nature hates a vacuum, the sheepherders moved in, started taking things over. You have to wonder about them to begin with. Here they are starting off where we finished, everything took us so long to get they have right away. They're sad more than anything . . . sadder than the old-timers moving south. You know what these kids who stayed on Long Island know? Shopping centers, that's it. If it's not in a mall they don't know nothing. And talk about dreams, they don't have any. A new stereo? A new Datsun? Call those dreams? Those aren't dreams, those are pacifiers. Popsicles. That's exactly what I feel like telling them. You find your own dream, pal, you're walking on mine. My generation survived the Depression, won the war, got Armstrong to the moon and back. And when I say *we* I'm talking about guys I know, not guys I read about. You think Grumman only makes F-14s? I *worked* on the landing module my last two years. Me, Tommy DiMaria. Nobody knows this but Scotty and me carved our initials on the facing under a transistor panel inside of the cabin. T.DM.S.S.H. right straight to the goddamn moon. But that's the kind of thing *we* did. What will the sheepherders be able to say they did when they get to be our age? . . . Evaded the draft. Bought a Cougar. Jogged.

It's like I told each of my kids when they were teenagers. "This town is where you grow up," I told them, "not where you *end* up." And they didn't either. They're scattered all over the place. I'm proud of them all. The only problem is like when Kathy got sick the last time it was a hell of a job getting everyone together. When I think about Kathy dying you know what I remember? Kennedy Airport. The TWA terminal. Going there to meet each of the kids, trying to figure out plane schedules, time zones, who I'm seeing off, who I'm meeting. The older I get the more I think what the real problem is in this country isn't *what* or *how* or *why* but *where*. *Where's* the question, the country's so goddamn big. Where in hell do you put yourself in it? Where?

Each of the kids wanted me to move in with them after Kathy died. Candy's a psychologist, she told me I was crazy to live by myself in the suburbs. If it was one thing people in suburbs couldn't stand it was to see someone living alone. It threatened them, they'd do anything to get rid of that reminder the world wasn't created in minimum denominations of two . . . that's the way she talks. But I told her no because the very last thing Kathy said was, Tommy, whatever you do don't give up the house. She was holding my hand, it was late, I was there all by myself not even a nurse. "Tommy, don't give up the house!" "Shh, Kathy," I whispered. "Rest now. I won't ever give it up." She squeezed my hand. I looked around to see if the nurse had come in, but it wasn't her, it was the lady in the next bed mumbling something in

12   her sleep. "I'll never give it up, Kathy," I promised. I bent over. I kissed her. She smiled . . . she closed her eyes and it was like she had gone to sleep.

"Goodbye, Kathy," I said. "Sweet dreams, princess."

It was harder without her. I remember I'm in the back yard fixing up the garden for spring just like I would if she was still there, watching Ginger out of the corner of my eye, when Mapes's wife comes up the driveway. She stands there chewing gum. "I'm sorry about your wife, Mr. DiMaria," she says. "I guess you're going to sell your house now, huh? " When I told her no she acted mad. "We'll see about that!" she says.

Her little boy Ringo runs over to help me like he sometimes did. She pulls him away, stands there clutching him tight to her body like she's protecting him. "Never play with that dirty old man again!" she screams. "You old people think you can keep putting us down all the time! You think you can ask anything for a house we'll pay it on account of we're desperate! What's Janey supposed to do, live in Queens the rest of her life?" She's screaming, getting all worked up. Mapes comes over, looks embarrassed, tries to quiet her down . . . away they go.

A few days later I'm out there again, this time planting beans, when I hear voices coming from the porch. I'm just about to go inside to investigate when this guy in a suit comes around back with a young couple holding hands. "This is the yard!" he says, pointing. "It's a nice yard, good place for kids. Hello doggy, what's your name?" He walks around me like I'm not there, squeezes a tomato, leads them back around front. Ten minutes later they come out of the house. "You'll like it here, it's a good investment. Oh, hello," he says, "you must be the owner. I'm Mr. Charles from Stroud Realty, here's my card, these are the Cana-days, they love your house." "Scram!" All three of them jump. "Go on, you heard me! Clear the hell out before I call the

cops!""But I'm showing the property!" the little guy squeaks. I
had a hell of a time chasing them off of there.

The pressure really started after that. It was little ways at first.
Kids that had been friendly before staying away because their
mothers told them to. Finding my garbage can spilled across the
lawn. Mail stolen, things like that. One morning there's a knock
on the door, this pimple face is standing there holding a briefcase.
"Mr. DiMaria?" "That's right, who are you?" "I'm from the
county. We've come to assess your home." "It was assessed." He
looks at his chart. "Yes, but twenty years ago. I'm sure it still can't
be worth just four thousand now can it? Excuse me." He butts his
way in, starts feeling the upholstery. He's there five minutes, he
comes back to the door. "Nice place you got here, Mr. DiMaria. I
can see you put a lot of work into it since we were last here. Let's
say forty thousand dollars' worth, shall we? Your taxes will be
adjusted accordingly."

"You're crazy!" I yell. I'm about to lose my temper but then I
remember something. "Hey, you know D'Amato down at the
county executive's office? Him and me grew up together." "Never
heard of him," pimple face says, shaking his head. "Well, how
about Gus Louis in the sheriff's office? " "Oh, we don't have much
to do with them these days I'm afraid." He starts to leave. "Well,
you're probably going next door now, right?" "Oh, no," he says.
"This is the only house on the block we're checking." "Wait a
second!" I yell. "That's bullshit. You're going to Mapes, then Silver
or I'm calling my congressman. Discrimination's a crime, pal!" His
eyes finally light up. "You mean Mr. Silver? Hell of a nice guy. His
brother is my boss. Goodbye, Mr. DiMaria. Have a nice day."

I don't want to give the impression I didn't fight back. I did,
because if there's one thing I know about Levittown it's this.
People are scared about blacks moving in, only nowadays it isn't
blacks, it's drug treatment centers. It terrifies everyone. It terrifies

14 them because all they think about when they're not shopping is property values. So what does DiMaria do? I wait until the next time these sweet Seventh Day whatever ladies come around selling their little pamphlets. I always give them a dime, no one else on the street ever gives them a penny . . . they think the world of me. They're always very polite, a bit crazy. What I did when they rang the doorbell was invite them into the house for some coffee. That was probably enough to give most of the sheepherders a good scare. It's Saturday, they're all out waxing their Camaros, here's two black ladies inside DiMaria's talking about God knows what, maybe thinking to buy it. But what I do is take them outside around back saying I wanted to show them my peach tree. These ladies are so sweet and polite, they're a bit deaf, besides they'll do anything I want.

I point to the side of the house. "This is where we'll put the rehabilitation room!" I say really loud. "Over here we'll have the methadone clinic!" The ladies are nodding, smiling, handing me new pamphlets, I'm slipping them fresh dimes. "AND OVER HERE'S THE ABORTION WING!" I see Mapes and Silver staring at us all upset; if they had a gun they would have shot me.

What really kept me going, though, was Hank Zimmer. He was the last cowboy left besides me. Every once in a while I'd get discouraged, he'd cheer me up, then he'd get discouraged, I'd cheer him up . . . we'd both get discouraged, we'd take it out working on my new den, maybe his. What we used to talk about was how there were no hedges on Lindbergh in the old days, no fences, no locked doors. Everyone's home was your home; we all walked back and forth like it was one big yard.

That was long since done with now. You think the sheepherders would have anything to do with the other sheepherders? It was like the hedges we'd planted, the bushes and trees, had grown up so high they'd cut people off from each other. The only thing they wanted anymore was to pretend their neighbors weren't there.

I remember the last time he came over because it was just after I finished wallpapering the den. Ginger was whining to go out so I let her . . . that crap about leashes didn't bother me at all. Hank's telling me about school taxes going up again, how he didn't think he could pay his on social security, nothing else. "What we should do," he says, "is find other people in our position to organize a senior citizens' group to see if something can't be done." "Hank," I tell him, "no offense or anything, but all of that what you just said is pure phooey. You join one of those senior citizens' groups, women's groups, queer groups, right away you put yourself in a minority, you're stuck there. All these people running around wanting to be in a minority just so they can feel all nice and persecuted. Forget it! We're humans, that puts us in the *majority!* We're humans, we should demand to be treated like it."

Hank runs his hands up and down the wallpaper, admires the job. "Yeah, you're probably right," he says. Humans. He never thought of it that way before. We go into the kitchen for some coffee. "Now what my idea is, we find out where Big Bill Levitt is these days, we get a petition together telling him how things have gone wrong here, all these young people moving in, taxes going up, forcing us out. He'll find some way to make things right for us. I'd stake my life on it."

Hank nods, reaches for the cream. "By the way," he says. "You hear about Johnny Holmes over on Hillcrest? The guy who once broke his chin on the high board at the pool?" "What about him?" "He's moving to Fort Lauderdale, him and his wife. They bought this old house there. They're going to fix it up nice. Have a garden and all. He made it sound very appealing." "Oh, yeah?" I say. Then I remember myself. "Appealing, my ass. It'll collapse on him, he'll be back in a month. If you don't mind my saying so, Hank, change the subject before I throw up."

16   All of a sudden we hear this godawful roar from out front like a car accelerating at a drag strip, then brakes squealing, only I knew right away it wasn't brakes. "Ginger!" I jump up, knock the coffee over, run outside . . . There's this car fishtailing away up the street. In the middle of the pavement in a circle from the streetlight is poor Ginger. I run over, put her head in my lap, pet her, but it's too late, she's crying, kicking her legs up and down. Behind her head's nothing but blood. Hank's next to me nearly screaming himself . . . There's nothing to do but put her out of her pain with my bare hands because there's no other way. Then Hank's got his arm around me, I'm shivering, crying, cursing, all at the same time. He takes me back to the house, his wife comes over, they have me swallow something . . . the next thing I know it's morning, Hank's buried Ginger in the back near the birch tree she always liked to curl up against in the sun.

It was a while before I found out who did it. I kept on taking my walk around the block same as before, except I didn't have Ginger with me anymore. Maybe a month later I'm walking along past Silver's house, I see him out in his driveway with Mapes, a few other sheepherders. Silver is giggling. Mapes is standing to one side acting half-ashamed, but smirking, too. "Hey, DiMaria!" Silver yells. "How's your dog?"

I didn't do anything right away. We had a tradition in the old days, you had a score to settle you took your time. I waited for the first stormy night, went over there with two buckets of the cheapest red paint money could buy.

It was pretty late. I shined a flashlight at the lampost which if you ever want to try it is enough to put one of those mercury vapor jobs out of commission for a while. Then I propped my ladder against the side of his house facing Mapes, went to work. The first cross stroke on the left was pretty easy, the upper right-hand one was tougher because I had to paint across a bay window

O'Brien had put in years before. I was being careful not to drip
any on the bushes. No matter what I thought of Silver I had a
certain amount of respect for his shrubbery which had been
planted by Big Bill Levitt back in the forties. It must have taken me
two hours all told. I'm painting away humming to myself like it
was something I did every night. When it was morning I woke up
early, took my usual stroll past Silver's house, there on the side
looking wet and shiny in the sun is the biggest, ugliest, coarsest
swastika you ever saw, painted right across the side of his house
big as life, the only thing bothered me was the upper right stroke
was a bit crooked after all.

There were pictures of it in the paper, editorials saying Levittown had gone to hell which was true but for the wrong reasons.
The entire Island's gone sour if you ask me. The Sound's gone
sour, the ocean's gone sour, the dirt's gone sour. We used to grow
enough tomatoes to last the winter, these great big red ones, now
you're lucky if you get enough to feed the worms. Great South
Bay? Sick clams, dead scallops, that's it. I remember it wasn't that
long ago we used to catch stripers bigger than a man's arm, me
and Scotty, right off Fire Island a twenty-minute drive away. I
remember going there before dawn, cooking ourselves breakfast
over a fire we made from driftwood, not seeing another soul on
the beach . . . just Scotty, me, the sun, the stripers. Nowadays?
Nowadays you can't even fish without getting your reel gummed
up in oil; you're lucky to take one crap-choked blowfish let alone
stripers.

Looking back what I think happened was that guys like
Scotty, Buzz, Mike, and me had the right dream in the wrong
place. Long Island's gone sour. Sometimes I remember the first
day I came out here, a know-nothing kid, watching that farmer,
that last old farmer up there on that overloaded Chevy looking
around saying good-bye at the same time cursing it once for all.
Other times I walk around the house looking for something to

do. What I usually end up doing is put the record player on. Mitch Miller doing "Exodus." I put it on real loud. When they sing, "This land is mine, God gave this land to me," I start singing, too. Listening to it makes me feel stronger, so I keep turning it up, playing it again. After that I fix lunch for myself. Tuna fish, a cup of soup. After lunch I end up staring out the front window trying to figure out who lived where in the old days. Know something? It gets harder every year. O'Brien's and Scotty's are easy, but sometimes I get confused on the others.

It's like this morning I'm looking out across the street trying to remember if Buzz or Rich Ammons lived where this sheepherder name of Diaz lives now, when who do I see over on Zimmer's lawn but the same real estate bastard I chased off my place, Mr. Charles, with two young kids showing them around. This time I was really mad. I ran outside without even a coat, started screaming at them, telling them I'd call the cops, break every bone in his miserable little body if he didn't clear out and leave poor Hank alone. But what happened next was that Hank was outside, too. He was pleading with me to stop, but by then it was too late. Real estate man and kids are running into their car, locking the doors, racing away.

"Tommy!" Hank yelled, shaking his head. "They were going to pay me fifty-five thousand, Tommy!" "What are you talking about?" But now he looked away like he was ashamed. He took me inside the sun porch, sat me down on a lawn chair he unhooked from the wall.

"Tommy, we're moving south," he said. "Bullshit you are!" But he doesn't do anything, he just sits there. "We can't take it here anymore, Tommy, " he whispered. "The cold gets to Marge. The taxes are too much for me. All those kids, what do we have in common with them? We're going to Florida. Saint Pete. We bought a trailer."

It was probably the next to worse moment I ever had. "You can't do that, Hank," I said, just as quiet as him. "Not after what we've been through all these years. I was going to help you out with your den. Think of all the things we could do yet. There's another porch we could add on, we could add on a pool." But he was shaking his head again. "Let's face it, " he said. "You've got nothing left to work on, Tommy. The house is finished. You hear me? Finished! There's nothing left." He took out his wallet, showed me some pictures. "My grandkids. Terri and Shawn. They live down there now. We want to be close to them. That's the main reason, Tommy. We want to be close to them the years we have left."

By now I was getting mad. "Grandkids my ass!" I yelled. "You think your grandkids give a damn about you? Maybe at Christmastime, that's it. To them you're an old smelly man they don't give a damn about they never will. Take it from me, I know." But then I looked at him . . . seeing him blink, cover his face with his hands, I got feeling ashamed of myself. "Hank," I said, "don't leave me alone like this. Please, Hank. Just hold on a little while more."

"Fifty-five thousand, Tommy. I can't turn it down."

"Listen, Hank. We'll call Big Bill Levitt up. I'll say, Mr. Levitt, my name is Tommy DiMaria, I live on Lindbergh Street, you probably don't remember but you once let me have a house for eighty-three dollars down instead of a hundred. Remember that, Mr. Levitt? Remember those days? Well, a lot of us old-timers are having trouble hanging on to our places you built for us. We wondered if maybe you could help us out. We'll call him up, Hank. We'll call him up just like that."

"You and your Levitt! I'm sick of hearing about him! What has Levitt ever done? He built these places and never looked back. He made his pile, then didn't want to know nothing. Levitt? You're so crazy about Levitt, let me ask you something. Where is Levitt now? Tell me that. Where is he now? Where is Levitt now?"

20   Like a dope, like the idiot I am, I shake my head, whisper, "I don't know, Hank. Where?"

"Florida!"

"Hank," I said, "I hope you fry."

When I got back to my place there was a panel truck in front, two men standing on the sidewalk watching me cross the street. At the same time Mapes's wife is on her lawn pointing at me, yelling "That's him, officer! That's your man!" One of the men came up to me the moment I reached the curb. "You Thomas A. DiMaria?" he said. "Beat it!" "You live at 155 Lindbergh?" "Beat it! You're trespassing on private property, pal!" "We're from the electric company. This is for you."

I'm feeling so tired by then I took the envelope, opened it up. Inside is a bill for $11,456.55. "You owe us for thirty-two years' worth," the man said. "If we want we can put you in jail. Stealing electricity is a crime." I looked back toward Mapes's house, sure enough there he is with that same half-ashamed smirk hiding behind his Cougar pretending he's polishing the roof.

"I'm not paying," I said. "Leave me alone." With that the other man, the one who hadn't said anything before, comes right up to me, waves a paper in my face. "You better pay, DiMaria!" he said with a sneer. "You don't, we take the house!"

I didn't waste any time after that. I went out to the tool shed, took a five-gallon can of gasoline, went back inside . . . took off the cap, taped a piece of cheesecloth over the spout, went into the den.

Sprinkle, sprinkle. Right over the desk. Sprinkle. Right over the wallpaper. Then after that I went into the bathroom. I remembered those men putting it in. I remembered redoing it with a bigger tub, new tiles, new cabinets. Sprinkle, sprinkle. Right over the cabinets. Right over the rugs. Next I went up the stairs I'd built with Scotty from lumber we helped ourselves to at a construction project on the turnpike . . . up to the dormer I'd added on for the

kids. Their stuff was still there, all the kids' stuff, because they
didn't want it, Kathy would never let me throw it away. There's a
blue teddy bear called Navy, a brown one called Army. I took the
can, poured some over their fur, propped them up in the corner,
poured some over the bunk beds. I remembered the time Candy
cried because she had the bottom one, she wanted the top. Thinking about that, thinking about the times I sat around the old
DuMont watching Mickey Mouse Club with them waiting for
Kathy to get home, almost made me stop right there.

I went downstairs, the can getting lighter, leaving a little trail
behind me . . . into the twins' room where I sprinkled some on
the curtains Kathy sewed, sprinkled some on the Davy Crockett
hat Chris used to wear every time she came out of the bathtub.
Then after that I went into the kitchen. The kitchen cabinets. The
linoleum. Sprinkle, sprinkle. Out to the porch where we used to
eat in summer, right over the bar I made from leftover knotty
pine. I stood there for a while. I stood there remembering the
party we had when we ripped the mortgage up, how Scotty got
drunk and we had to carry him home only we carried him,
dropped him in the pool instead. Sprinkle, sprinkle. Like watering
plants. Like baptizing someone. Like starting a barbecue with
lighter fluid, all the neighborhood there in my back yard. Into our
bedroom, over the floor, the floor where the first night I brought
Kathy home we had no bed yet so we lay there on the floor of
what we still couldn't believe was our house, making love all night
because we were so happy we didn't think we could stand it.
Sprinkle. The fumes getting pretty bad now. Sprinkle. Outside to
the carport, over the beams, over the tools, over everything.
Sprinkle, sprinkle. Splash.

And that's where I am right now. The carport. The bill they
handed me in one hand, a match in the other. I'm going to wait
until Silver gets home first. I want to make sure everyone on the
block gets to see what fifty-five thousand dollars, thirty-two years,

22   looks like going up in smoke. A second more and it'll be like kids,
       neighbors, house, never happened, as if it all passed in a twin-
       kling of an eye like they say. One half of me I feel ready to start all
       over again. I feel like I'm ready to find a new dream, raise a new
       family, the works. Nothing that's happened has made me change
       my mind. I'm ready to start again, just say the word. I feel
       stronger, more hopeful than ever . . . how many guys my age can
       say that? That's all I want, one more chance. For the time being
       I'm moving back to the old neighborhood to my sister's. After
       that, I don't know. Maybe I'll head down south where it's
       warmer, but not, I repeat NOT to Florida, maybe as far as
       Virginia, I'm not sure.

If a Woodchuck Could Chuck Wood

THEY had lasagna for Thanksgiving dinner that year. The meatless kind. From a can.

"Nothing like the smell of a good bird in the oven," Mike Senior announced, scraping his boots on the doormat, inhaling.

"Uh, Pop?" Janet whispered.

"Yes, ma'am?"

"Never mind. Happy Thanksgiving, Pop. Let me help you with your coat. There are a few things in the kitchen I've got to see to yet. Mike should be back any minute. I'll leave you and Shawn to get reacquainted."

He smelled it all morning. He smelled it when he woke up in the cramped, stuffy bedroom he rented near the school in South Boston where he worked as a custodian part-time—fresh, brought in from the woodshed where it had been kept during the night to keep it moist. He smelled it as the bus crossed the state line into Maine—skin turning brown, the first drippings running down the sides. He smelled it at the rest stop where he bought Shawn an Indian tomahawk made in Taiwan, smelled it during the walk from the abandoned railroad bridge where the bus let him off— almost done now, the gravy bubbling in the pan, its aroma taking him past the boarded-up stores of the old mill town, the over-grown orchards, the brief view of the lake which meant he was halfway there . . . a rich, fragrant distillation of sixty Thanksgivings past, so strong that none of the changes in the house could

24   stain it; not the plastic stretched tight over the windows to keep out drafts, not the towels stuffed against cracks the plastic missed, not the ugly black woodstove jutting out from the fireplace, appropriating all the space near the couch . . . not even the garlic and parmesan cheese Janet was sprinkling over the top of the casserole dish in a last desperate attempt to make it all palatable.

"And just how heavy is it this year, Shawn?" he asked, playing to memories and traditions he felt it was his duty to impart.

"Seven. Seven and a half in May."

Shawn was busy chopping up the coffee table. He thought his grandfather had asked him his age.

"Seven pounds, eh? Kind of on the scrawny side, isn't it? By the way, Shawn. That's a real Indian scalping hatchet you've got yourself there. Never point it at anybody unless you mean business."

Mike got home around one. He didn't say where he had been. He went into the bathroom to wash his hands.

"I was just admiring your stove there," Mike Senior said when he came back. "Clever the way it fits in so snug."

"Eats wood."

Mike Senior nodded, as if Mike had said something profound. "That so? Well, guess it's nice to have the trusty furnace to fall back on. You can say what you want about the good old days but give me a nice tight burner every time."

"We shut it off, Pop. Eats oil."

Mike Senior nodded again, pursing his lips this time, as if his son had just topped his previous insight with an even truer one. "That's an idea. Hey, you know, talking about woodstoves . . . We used to have one when I was a boy. A real potbelly, too. At least my grandfather did. He was quite a piece of work, my grandfather. Your great-grandfather, Mike. Shawn's great-great-grandfather. It was my job to fill the stove every night before I went to bed so it wouldn't go out."

"Did it?"

"Did it what?"

"Go out. This one's always going out. That's what it does best. Goes out."

"Well, naturally. You've got to . . ." He tried to remember what his grandfather had said in 1918. "You've got to spit on it first. You've got to make sure your tinder is dry."

Mike sat on the couch nursing a beer. His face had hardened since the last time Mike Senior had seen him. There was something reproachful about his prematurely gray hair, his tired eyes. "You never showed me, Pop. You never taught me about woodstoves when I was small."

It took Mike Senior off guard. The frowning. The green work pants he hadn't bothered changing out of. He wished Shawn would come back from wherever he was hiding. "Well, no. Of course, because we didn't have one. We had a furnace, Mike. I remember showing you where the oil went in. Remember, Mike? It was through the spigot underneath your mother's rhododendron."

"Was that the same grandfather whose brother starved to death on his way out West?"

"He didn't starve," Mike Senior said angrily. "At least he did, but it wasn't his fault. The wagon train lost its way. Their scout was drunk. It was an unusually bad winter."

He didn't like the direction the conversation was heading. Not at all. He waited until Janet came in, then—following the ritual—sniffed at the air like a bird dog, glanced significantly at the pocket watch he had bought at Woolworth's to someday leave to Shawn, pushed himself up off the couch.

"Guess it's time I started working on the old gobbler," he said, stretching. "Got my favorite knife all sharpened up for me, Janet?"

"Uh, Pop?"

But it was too late. Before Janet could stop him he had gone into the kitchen.

26   "Please, Pop. Don't say anything to Mike about it, okay? He's super uptight about things right now. He's discouraged, Pop. You would be too if you were in his shoes. Let's just have a nice quiet dinner for a change, all right? All right, Pop?"

He heard Janet whispering all this over his shoulder, he saw the casserole dish cooling off on the counter, saw the rubbery noodles the color of slugs, the blistered tomato sauce, the black stains in the empty oven, but it still didn't register. He stood there rubbing his nose in disbelief.

"What's this?" he finally managed to choke out.

"It's called lasagna, Pop. It's Italian food. We thought we'd try something different this year."

"Something cheaper you mean," Mike said. He was in the kitchen now, pushing Shawn out in front of him. "Shawn wants to see Grandpop carve."

But Mike Senior had recovered himself now. He started digging away at the middle of it with Janet's spatula, ignoring his son's sarcasm. "Who wants an end piece? Shawn? Nice crispy corner going to waste here. Nothing like variety I always say. Variety is the spice of life. Nice dark piece okay for you, Janet?"

He carried the dish into the dining room, trying to hide his disappointment. It was one tradition down, but there was another yet to go. All during the bus drive he had rehearsed saying grace, going over different words, trying them out on the bus driver who was glad for the company and helpful in suggesting phrases of his own. It was a special prayer for the occasion, traditionally reverential but timely, too, showing Mike he understood after all. He was too shy to tell him so face-to-face, but with all their heads bowed he thought he might just bring it off.

"I think we're ready to start now, Mike," he said, interrupting the celery before it could be passed any further. "Heavenly father . . ."

But Mike missed his cue—whether deliberately or accidentally,

Mike Senior couldn't tell. He was talking to Shawn, jabbing his fork at the casserole dish like a teacher pointing to a map. "We can't have turkey anymore, Shawn. Why not?"

Shawn didn't answer.

"Because it's too expensive, that's why not. It costs over a dollar a pound and lasagna feeds the four of us for only a buck. Understand that, Shawn?"

"Why bother him with it?" Janet said. She had seen her father-in-law fold his hands, then quickly unfold them, and she felt embarrassed.

"The boy has to learn," Mike said defensively, putting his fork back down. "The sooner he does, the easier it'll be."

They finished dinner in silence. Mike Senior wondered if it would be possible to slip grace in before dessert, but as it turned out there wasn't any dessert, only coffee. By the time they finished and washed the plates off—they didn't use the dishwasher anymore, Janet explained—it was still only three. Janet said something about Parchesi. Mike said something about needing more wood.

"That's the best idea I've heard all day. Mind if an old man tags along?"

Mike went to find Shawn who was hiding again, this time in the bathroom. He stood over him while he buttoned his coat. He made him leave his tomahawk behind on the kitchen counter. "This isn't a game, Shawn. If you work hard you can play with it later."

Janet was watching the three of them get ready from the sink. He turned to her, heading off her protest before it was made. "Well, it isn't, you know. Not anymore. The boy has to learn."

They went through the door in chronological order—Shawn in a hurry to be outside, Mike Senior hanging back to fasten his hood, Mike . . . dressed in the army jacket that had always been too short for him, even in the army . . . caught somewhere in

28   between, needing to free himself of the house, feeling reluctant to face the cold. It was below freezing now. The sun had lost its strength in nagging its way westward through the iodine-colored clouds which had clung to it since morning; what yellow was left was wasted on the roof of the corrugated iron shed where he kept his tools. He crawled in on his hands and knees, then shoved out what they would need. An oil can and some rags. The chain saw. Almost as an afterthought, the ax.

"Let me give you a hand with that, Shawn."

"Don't, Pop. He can manage."

"Yeah, but it's awfully heavy, Mike. I just thought . . ."

"I know what you thought, Pop."

There was no use arguing with him. Mike Senior gathered up what was left, then hurried after them, his irritation soothed away by the ax. He felt it only fitting that he should be the one to carry it. When Mike first handed it to him, he had swung it back and forth to check its balance, then held it outstretched in front of him to sight down the shaft. "Good ax," he announced at last, running an appreciative finger along the blade. "Damn good ax."

The path crossed a culvert, then merged into an overgrown dirt road the construction crews had used in putting up the summer houses around the lake back in the fifties. There were *No Trespassing* signs here, the remains of a wire fence once rumored to be electrified. Mike stepped over it into the trees, or at least what was left of them. A worm had gotten all the pine. There were still some birch but not many. The summer people cut them down to decorate their fireplaces.

"Up here!"

He saw the two of them cross the stream in the wrong direction, then swerve back toward the road. His father had caught up with Shawn now. He was saying something to him, helping him with the saw. He carried the ax the wrong way, propped over his shoulder like a rifle. Trip over a stone and it's goodbye ear, Mike thought, lighting a cigarette. He wondered what he was telling Shawn.

There was a dead tree on the edge of the woods. Maple, possibly oak. He couldn't tell without the leaves. He had discovered it the same afternoon he lost his job—rotten, tilting, but not yet down. It hadn't meant much to him at first. Something noticed through the bitterness, nothing more. But as October went by and his walks became longer, he began to feel the tree was deliberately mocking him by staying upright, the same way the neat, unused woodpiles of the summer people mocked his own empty shed, his stove that ate wood, then went out. Finally, the night before, lying next to Janet unable to sleep, he heard a distant thump up near the lake, as if a giant had suddenly drummed his fist against the frozen ground. He nodded—for the first time in weeks he allowed himself to smile.

"Whew. You set a pretty good pace there, Mike," his father said, swinging the ax off his shoulder, missing his ankle by a hair. "This is our baby, eh? Nice sturdy elm from the look of her. Where shall we dig in?"

Mike ignored him. He took the chain saw from Shawn and opened the gas tank to make sure it was full. He pushed the prime in twice, then yanked the starter cord out much harder than was necessary. "Damn."

Mike Senior was breaking off some branches near the tree's base. Shawn was straddling the trunk, kicking his heels up and down like a cowboy. Neither one had seen him.

"Get off of there, Shawn!" he yelled automatically, wondering what in hell could be wrong. He pulled it again, breaking the cord this time, the little knob on the end flying backwards into his face.

The saw burped—there was a gratifying cloud of blue smoke, then a roar. He was shouting for them to get out of the way . . . he was fighting to hold the saw steady, bracing it against his thigh the way the salesman had showed him in the store . . . when it

30 burped again, throwing sparks out from beneath the handle, kicking loose from his hands, and somersaulting across the dead tree onto the ground. It spun violently around the underbrush for what seemed like minutes, sending branches and pine needles and pebbles into the air in a miniature whirlwind before conking out against a rock.

None of them said anything. In the distance Mike could hear a small plane.

"Goddammit!"

It was Shawn who said it. Shawn who hadn't opened his mouth since they left the house. Mike Senior's face turned red—Mike drew back his hand as if to hit him. But he put it off for the time being. He squatted down next to the chain saw, prodding at it with a stick like someone checking to see whether a fierce animal was still alive.

"He picks it up at school," he said with a shrug once the safety was on. "Shawn! Say anything like that again you're going to get slapped, understand?"

The dead tree looked bigger now. There were branches poking out he hadn't noticed before, goiterlike knots where old limbs had broken off during storms, twisted vines that still held parts of the trunk dangerously high off the ground. With the chain saw he had thought it manageable, even puny. But now, unarmed, it was as if the tree were mocking him again—his broken saw, his joblessness, his son's mysterious silences and abrupt shouts.

"You pay a hundred bucks for something you'd think it would work," he said without much conviction.

Mike Senior nodded. "Good thing we have the ax."

He was swinging it back and forth like a batter limbering up on deck, the eagerness on his face contrasting with the sullenness on Shawn's, as if the two generations' usual roles had been reversed—Mike Senior the excited boy, Shawn the jaded old man.

"They didn't bother with fancy gizmos in the old days. All a man needed was an ax and a rifle and he was set for whatever came his way in life. They opened up a continent that way, Shawn. They made us the nation we are."

"Like Uncle whatshisname, right?" Mike said. "The guy who starved."

The stove ate kindling, not just logs. He showed Shawn what kind to look for and started him off through the trees with a little shove. He looked very small against the gray sky. Every now and then he would stoop down to pick up a stick, but it was obvious his heart wasn't in it. For a moment, Mike was tempted to call him back.

"First you make sure you got plenty of room to swing her . . ."

His father had taken his coat off. His father was rolling up his sleeves.

"Then you hold her nice and tight. Nice and tight, Mike. My grandfather had hands like a blacksmith. He'd take a tree like this and have it in toothpicks inside of a minute."

"Don't you think you better start further up?"

But he didn't listen. He spat on his hands, wiped them off on his pants, then brought the ax down with all his might against a huge knot in the tree's base. The blade glanced off without biting in, knocking some dirt loose, flaking off a few pieces of scabby bark.

"Nice and tight. I see what you mean."

Mike Senior shook his head in disbelief, staring at the ax like something must be wrong with it. He went over to the oil can and squirted some over the blade, then swung it again closer to the spot Mike suggested. This time the blade bit into the wood with a satisfyingly resonant whonk, but when he bent down to pry it loose for his next swing the ax refused to budge.

"It's stuck," he finally decided, after examining it from all angles. "Uh, your ax is stuck, Mike."

"So I see. What happens now?"

32   "I think it's your oil. They used to have this special kind years ago. I remember it came in a red, white, and blue can. It had Teddy Roosevelt's picture on the side. If we had some there'd be no problem."

"I thought you said you knew how to do it."

"I do. Only it's been a while, Mike. My grandfather wanted to show me, but my father wouldn't let him. He wouldn't let me go out in the woods once I was Shawn's age, Mike. He thought that was old-fashioned. People were ashamed to use wood in those days. We had a furnace. My father threw the ax out the day the men came and put it in."

He was still talking when Mike kicked the ax loose. Apologizing, explaining, making excuses for them both. But it was too late for that now—all Mike could think of was his own bitterness. He would hear his father's voice behind him as he brought the ax up, lose it beneath his own grunt as he slammed it back down, pick it up again as the hard, biting cut echoed off toward the lake.

"Things will get better, Mike. It might be kind of tough right now but you've got to keep the old chin up, roll with the punches."

He swung the ax harder, swinging it less at the tree than at all the frustration that had been building inside him for so long. Harder and harder. Deeper and deeper into the wood.

"Things always look darkest before the dawn, Mike. Things are bound to get better soon. I can feel better days in my bones."

The bosses. The unemployment office. The applications for work. The maybes. The next weeks. The sorrys. The nos. The staying home. The game shows. The walks. The Salvation Army store. The food stamps. The day-old pies. The making do, stretching out, diluting. Janet's own bitterness. The pipes that froze. The rags stuffed against drafts. The doctor's bills. The gas. The bare tires. The lottery tickets. The part-time jobs. The patches. The cutting back. The cold. The stove. The wood. The goddamn wood.

"It's free, Mike. That's the great thing about it. I heard the man say so on the radio this morning when I was getting ready to come."

Mike stopped to catch his breath. The sweat was rolling down his forehead, stinging his eyes. His wrist hurt—there was a pain in his back below his left shoulder. As tormenting as it was, his anger had made no visible impression on the dead tree. He was still less than a third of the way through.

"What?" he mumbled, feeling defeated.

"Energy from the sun, Mike. It's the energy of the future, the man said. It's our only renewable source of energy that's free."

Mike laughed. "Free, right? That's a good one, Pop. That's the best one I've heard in years. The sun, right? Somebody's already got a plan to slap a meter on it. They've probably got a patent on the thing right now. They're going to put it in a pump or a can and it's going to cost us plenty, you wait and see."

And when he turned to watch the sunset that's exactly how it looked—appropriated, sold, fading behind the ridge near the lake like all the other missed opportunities in his life, appealing only when gone. He was standing there watching it vanish when Shawn appeared from the same direction, blotting out his last glimpse of it, emerging from whatever faint light remained.

"Here he is!" Mike Senior yelled, happy for the distraction. "Our lumberjack, Mike. Look and see how much he's brought back."

"Too small."

"Here, take a look, Mike. He's got himself half the forest."

"Too small!"

Mike grabbed the branches from his son's arms and threw them toward the road. "Go back and find bigger ones, Shawn."

"Mike, for Pete's sake, he's only a . . ."

"Move!"

Shawn wiped his nose off on the sleeve of his coat, then started

34   robotlike in the opposite direction from the one he had come, pushing his way through the briars until he disappeared. Mike watched him go, then . . . grabbing the ax . . . swung it blindly at the dead tree with all the strength that was left in him. The bark flew up past his head . . . the tree shivered, writhed, began to split . . . the ax bit deeper, deeper . . . the overstrained shaft shattered apart into splinters, leaving a piece the size of a pencil sticking through his right hand.

"Mike!"

Without screaming, without saying a word, he dropped what was left of the broken ax and started running up through the woods toward the lake.

"Mike?"

Mike Senior went over to the tree to sit down, feeling drained, wondering whether he should wait for them there or go back to the house for help. It was dark out now. By squinting he could just make out the road, but not much further. He wasn't sure if he could find the way by himself—Mike wouldn't let Janet turn on the back spotlight anymore. He had just made up his mind to wait another ten minutes before shouting for them, when something small and square and silent separated itself from the black behind the tree.

"Shawn!"

He put both hands over his chest. He started shaking his head. "You gave me quite a start there, Shawn. Not good for the old ticker getting surprised like that. You could have been an Indian and what would I have done then?"

Shawn's arms were full. He came to a stop near the abandoned chain saw—mute, gloveless, staring up at his grandfather as if he had never really looked at him before.

"Uh, your Daddy's gone wee wee."

Shawn could tell his grandfather was embarrassed to be alone with him. He was fidgeting with his hands, clasping them to-

gether, then unclasping them, sliding his false teeth in and out
with his tongue in a way he never did when Shawn's parents were
around. At the same time he seemed on the point of saying something but not sure how to begin. He made Shawn come over and
sit down next to him. He patted his knee, then his shoulder. He
pointed to the broken ax, mumbled something about wagon trains
and grandfathers and not giving up. He made Shawn bow his
head like he did in Sunday school. He started reciting something
in a hoarse voice, like a frog's.

"Heavenly father . . ."

The words were too big for Shawn—he was too busy studying
his grandfather's face to pay attention. He kept his eyes closed
most of the time, but every so often he would stop mumbling long
enough to look nervously over his shoulder toward the lake,
reminding Shawn of a squirrel.

". . . and for our health which has been pretty good all things
considered, and for this thy produce of thy table . . ."

On and on. Louder and louder. There was a dab of spit on his
lips. There was a little gray froth churned up when they moved.

". . . we await thy assistance, thanking you serenely for pitch-
ing in to help like you have, bestow . . . upon . . ."

He lost his way, doubling back over words Shawn knew he had
already said, stopping, shutting his eyes even tighter as though he
was trying to squeeze them out.

"Bestow . . . grateful, Lord . . . thy humble servants . . ."

He was mumbling again when Shawn's father came back. He
was in one of the intervals where his eyes were closed so he didn't
see what Shawn saw—that his father's right hand was wrapped in
a dirty handkerchief, that his father was carrying an armful of
wood.

"Where are they?" he demanded.

Six logs. White, evenly cut. Six logs of magical white birch.

"Too green," he said, kicking apart Shawn's pile of kindling

36 with his boot. But he said it halfheartedly—the kick was misdirected, more like a shrug than a kick. He seemed in a hurry, glancing back toward the lake the same way Shawn's grandfather had while saying his prayers.

"The boy has to learn," he said to no one in particular, handing Shawn one of the birch logs, then another, then a third. It was all Shawn could do to hold them. He felt his knees give way under the weight—he bit his tongue to keep from crying.

"Let's get out of here." His father grabbed the chain saw and started running down toward the house.

"I'll help you," his grandfather whispered, holding back. "He can't see us now. Here, let me take this heavy one off the top."

They made their way through the woods as best they could, tripping over stones, sliding on dead leaves. His grandfather kept whispering words Shawn couldn't understand, his breath feeling hot and tickly, stinking of garlic. Shawn tried to block it out, slapping at his ear like it was a mosquito which wouldn't go away, thinking only of how much he hated the wood he carried in his arms. How he hated the scabby feel of it. How he hated its smell when it burned—the way its smell associated itself with everything in life he had learned to detest.

"I promise, Shawn."

He wouldn't listen now. The dark. The cold. It seemed he had always been tumbling through it this way, arms aching, wrists scratched and bleeding. It seemed he always would be, too, forever trying to catch up, unable to escape a future consisting entirely of heavier logs, even thicker, more acrid smoke.

"Things will get better, Shawn."

His father was waiting for them by the house, the spotlight turned on after all, throwing his shadow out across the lawn like a giant's.

"Things will get better!" his grandfather hissed as they stepped clear of the woods, piling the third log back on top of the two he

already carried so his father wouldn't know. But it was too much
for Shawn. The weight. The unfairness. From all the frustration
and fear he finally found the word he had been groping for all
afternoon.

"Liar!"

He spun around to face his father, throwing up his arm to
protect himself from the inevitable slap. But his father's expression never changed. His father was looking down at the
ground pretending not to have heard—his father was falling
down onto his knees, gathering in the logs Shawn had dropped
with a furious scooping of his arms. In that one glimpse Shawn
knew that he had won—that his father would never stop him
now, that he could yell at his grandfather again.

"Liar!" he screamed, hating him. "Liar!"

The Lob

I F Richard Uncle Richard were a tennis shot, it would almost
certainly be a lob. Tall, balloon-faced at thirty-four, he
seemed, as he sat fussing with his racket off to the shady
side of the patio, like someone drifting into an imminent and not
particularly difficult smash.

"I have an announcement, everyone!" June said, swinging a fly
swatter playfully past his head as though she were just the person
to make it.

Richard didn't move. If he made a good lob in the literal sense,
he made an even better one in the figurative one. A lob is a
hopeful shot and for years Richard had been the hope of the
Mansfields—wavering, subject to unforseeable and dismaying
gusts, but their hope nevertheless, flung up in the air October 12,
1948 as Richard Martin the Third, with all the expectation and
calculated aim it implied. Even now—his father dead, his mother
confined to the mainland with cancer, surrounded as he was by
nieces and nephews and guests he no longer knew, the rather
pathetic keeper of family traditions no one else remembered, the
intruder on new traditions he couldn't seem to catch up with,
arrived for the first weekend in six summers without a tennis
partner of his own—even now, with all these things, it would
have been very hard for any of them to pinpoint exactly where on
the trajectory he was.

Still rising up easily and confidently off the racket? He was only in his thirties, he was in good shape yet, with most of life still before him. At the apogee now, poised above them all with the ultimate landing point already determined but still to be revealed? He felt that way, felt right up on top of things, with some of his early momentum gone but with plenty more to look forward to on the way down. Or was it down? Seeing the Scotch in the wine glass near his sneaker, listening to the way he cursed the tennis racket because the stringing job was botched again—was it down? Was it down, and if it was down, would he be landing well within the baseline for a point, or just out, an inch or two long?

The lob, his nieces called him. Richard Uncle Richard. But he didn't really mind—in fact, it rather flattered him. Tennis was everything now and when his sister announced to the other guests on the patio that she was pregnant his only reaction was to wonder what its effect would be on the afternoon's game.

"None whatsoever," June said when he finally got her alone near the garden. "I don't even show yet. Aren't you going to congratulate me?"

"It's not as if it never happened before."

"Thank you."

"Okay. Congratulations," and he bent down to give her a quick kiss on the forehead. "Now that that's settled . . . I was watching Jack and Sue yesterday. It's her backhand we'll have to concentrate on. Jack tried to cover for her but it's still damn vulnerable."

"I want to talk to you," she said mysteriously.

"About what? About the game?"

She thought of him as an incurable dreamer, living half in the past. She probably always *had* thought of him that way, ever since the time he stopped being everyone's hero. But what was new that summer was the stuffy, condescending way she had of talking to him as though it were her duty to make him face the cold, hard facts of the world—the slow, grave shake of her head, as though what she had to tell him was too bitter for words.

"Richard," she would say, pursing her lips. "You're drinking too much Scotch."

"Oh, yeah right, June," he would answer, taking another sip. "Sure thing."

But this time before she could start in on him they were interrupted by Tommy who was on his way down to the beach with a half-inflated plastic dragon draped around his neck like a fur. Now that Bobby and Laurie were grown up, June had become sentimental over her younger ones—she couldn't bear seeing them go by without a hug.

"So talk," Richard said. In his role of doting uncle he had tried to puff the dragon up but his face turned red before any of the fins would stiffen.

"Later."

"I'm listening already."

"Later!" she said, tugging back Tommy's trunks to see how low his sunburn went. "Are you having lunch with everyone for a change?"

"Not now. Can't play on a full stomach, can I? Thought I'd hit a few serves while the court was still empty."

"Well, we have to talk, don't forget. Tommy likes the dragon you gave him Richard Uncle Richard, doesn't he Tommy dear?"

But she didn't wait for an answer. Kissing Tommy on the chin, shouting to Richard she'd be over after dessert, she took the dragon by the throat, puffed it up with one mighty puff, then disappeared back through the roses toward the house.

The tennis court was set high in a meadow above the sea. There were some burnt, toy-size pine trees for shade—a high fence on the ocean side to keep the balls from rolling in. To the road side, past the spot where his own Uncle Richard had his heart attack twenty years before, the dune grass began. By late August it was the same bleached, sandy color as the balls and the sharp blades

42 would cut apart the fuzz on any that bounced over. It was a rough court on balls. The temptation when you were mad was to blast one over the fence toward the sea, sending it skyward with all your might and seeing it plop into the water far offshore like little mortar shells or diving terns. You would feel your anger leave by the time the ball hit—feel it blown out in the sky, not doused in the water. Sometimes they flew over accidentally and whoever lost the set was expected to climb down the cliff and swim out after them.

Once they had been scrambling down when a harbor seal surfaced under the nearest and balanced it away on its nose, just the way seals did in circuses. Not the least of the resentments he had stored up against June was that in telling this story over the years she had somehow changed the seal to a shark.

"It *was* a shark," June insisted when he tried to correct her. They had staged the first of their famous shouting matches over it, sending the kids off in tears and ruining the afternoon's game.

And maybe it was a shark. Maybe Sue had really dumped coffee down their father's back that time, not lemonade. Maybe the weasel had actually been a squirrel. Maybe he had made up the legend of Sue's nighttime swim. June had everything else her own way now, she might as well have the memories.

It had been different when they were growing up. Those years it was Richard who was at the center of things. June and Sue were there but only peripherally somehow—hangers-on in a summer that revolved around him. Richard winning his fourth island championship in straight sets. Richard and his famous, ever-present harem. Richard in his incredible Dodge. Richard choosing the afternoon of June's reception to swan dive off the highest part of the cliff.

When it changed it changed so gradually he almost missed its significance. It was the summer after he left school, a month or so after he had quit his first job for reasons no one was quite clear about. He had been standing on the court waiting for the after-

noon's perpetual game to start up again when he caught sight of   43
June and her husband on the beach far below. They had their first
child Bobby with them—they had tied a clothesline around his
waist so he wouldn't drown. He was wading up to his knees while
his parents sat there on the beach holding one end, the rope from
that distance looking like the thin white string of a tea bag. Bobby
was kicking his legs back and forth in excitement, stirring up the
bottom until the water turned marble brown. For a moment Richard had been tempted to call out to them, get their attention
somehow, perhaps even dive off the cliff—backwards this time,
head over heels. But for some reason he didn't. For some reason
he suddenly knew that no one would particularly care if he did—
that in the course of one weekend and the next he had been
shunted aside to the summer's periphery in the same way he had
pushed June and Sue aside years before.

He didn't call out. Instead he hid behind one of the pine trees
and relieved himself against the needles. Down below, June and
Hank were kissing; from time to time they pulled Bobby back to
shore to make sure he was all right, as though the tea had steeped
long enough.

That same afternoon, for the first time anyone could remember,
he lost the match on straight double faults. The day after that he
tore a muscle in his thigh chasing a serve over the cliff. He had to
be helped aboard the ferry on crutches. It was five summers before he came back again, and by that time the summer routines
had changed out of all recognition. The beach was the center of
things—the tennis court had been resurfaced, but was hardly ever
used.

He would move out West, then halfway back again—get a pro-
motion or two, then get bored. Occasionally he sent them snap-
shots of the women he was going out with, all as beautiful as ever,
but looking very pale and helpless compared to the athletic, suntanned ones they remembered with him.

But as the years went by and Bobby and Laurie became old

enough to take lessons, tennis regained its former importance. That same summer Richard had moved back East for good, as though he had been waiting for that very thing all along. The old routines were dusted off, new ones created. He would arrive on the morning boat with whichever woman it was he'd invited for the weekend, tennis racket under his arm, the girl forced to carry the inflatable dragons and ponies and ships he'd brought for his nieces and nephews, the two of them starting on the long walk to the beach house because Richard was too impatient to wait for a ride. Hank would usually come upon them halfway with the jeep. They had a joke where he would beep his horn once if she was better looking than the one he had brought the week before, not beep at all if she wasn't.

Five weeks in a row he didn't beep. On the sixth—on the morning before—Richard had arrived all by himself, five different tennis rackets under his arm, but no presents this time, no embarrassed little smile, and no girl.

He measured the net with his hands to make sure Jack hadn't lowered it while he was away, then ran three quick laps around the court's circumference. He felt good about things, even though he was alone. What he felt especially good about was his serve. The lessons he'd been taking on his lunch hour were starting to pay off. It stayed fast and low, rattling to a stop against the fence where Tommy had hung his shell collection, enough steam left on the ball to knock even the biggest ones down the cliff.

He had finished serving the first bucket and was starting in on the second when June came over. She was by herself this time, dressed in what passed for her tennis outfit. Cutoffs, a T-shirt with a panda and the words "Love Me!" in the middle, purple and white wrist bands one of the girls had given her for Christmas. He had to admit she looked good in them, even with six kids behind her. And she could still play tennis. He was lucky to have her for a partner, he decided. At least with her he wouldn't have to worry about easing off on what Jack sarcastically referred to as "Richard's competitive fire." For a change he felt prepared to maintain his side of the truce. They had a few minutes yet—if she was interested he could even show her how to get more topspin on her serve.

"It's going to be a boy," she said, the moment she got up to him. He saw now she hadn't brought her racket with her, and he suddenly remembered her saying something about a talk.

"Yeah. Super congratulations, like I said."

Of course it would be a boy, now she had said so. She was famous for knowing ahead of time. Six babies and not once had she been wrong. No one was sure how she did it, not sure if it was a feeling she had down there, or some uncanny influence—simply a great feat of divination or some awesome power of design.

"It's going to be a boy," she said. "I'm going to name him Richard."

"The hell you are!" Richard yelled. He was so startled he dropped his racket in midswing.

"I'm going to name him Richard Martin Mansfield Lane the Fourth."

"The hell you are!" Richard yelled again, picking up the racket to see if any strings had torn.

"Why not?"

"It's my name, that's why not. You know the tradition."

"The tradition is that there's always one member of each generation named Richard Martin. We're talking about a new generation now, or hadn't you noticed?"

"The tradition is the *son* in the family names his own son that. It's my name to give and when I have a son he'll get it."

June gave the sorrowful little shake of her head, as though to

46   say she had been holding realism in reserve but hadn't wanted to use it.

"You'll never have a son," she said bluntly, "You're over thirty now and you'll never marry."

"Bullshit!"

She went on shaking her head as though she hadn't heard him—as though there were even more realism to come.

"You're over thirty and you'll never marry. It's time you realized it. There was a time there with Elaine when we all thought maybe you would, but . . ."

"I told you never to mention her."

"I want the name, Richard. There's no reason I need your permission, but you are family and I thought it would be polite on my part to ask you. It was your name at one time, that's true. But you've forfeited it. You haven't used it in time."

"You're insane!"

"I want the name."

"Give it to the next one!"

"There won't be a next one. This will be our last. Sue and Jack will be starting in soon. I want it before you give it to them."

"I'm not giving it to anyone. It's mine."

"Please, Richard?"

She would always switch from her maddening dogmatism to her little-girl-like pout. For a moment he might have had her, but in his anxiety to preserve the tennis game he made an even worse mistake of his own.

"Listen," he said. "If I'm not married in two years you can have it then, okay?"

"I want it now," she said, sensing he was weakening. "I talked it over with Hank on the phone this morning. You can be his godfather. We'll tell everyone that he was named after you."

"Forget it!"

"No."

"Yes!"

He knew from experience that if he didn't make some sort of compromise the argument was capable of staying here the entire afternoon, the two of them shouting "Yes!" and "No!" at each other as if sheer stubborn repeating of it could win where everything else had failed. He could see Jack and Sue coming toward them from the patio in their matching warm-ups—the game was due to start and he couldn't stand having anything go wrong.

"After the game, okay? We'll talk about it then. All I have to look forward to every week is the game here. It means a lot to me beating Jack after what he said the other night. Can't it please. . . . Can't it please, June, wait until later?"

She hesitated. He could see her look toward the patio and calculate how much time she had before the others reached them.

"I want that name, Richard," she whispered, but for the time being he had won. She reached down for one of his rackets to make it look like they had been practicing. "I want that name!" and picking up a loose ball, she drove it with a vicious swipe into the sea.

There were always two separate games to be played on that particular court, the one everybody could see and the one Richard played with himself in his memory. They were apt to have strange effects on each other. He would be chasing a shot up the sideline nearest the cliff and suddenly remember Uncle Richard's heart attack on that very spot in 1957. He would be almost up to the ball, would be drawing back his racket to smash it, when Uncle Richard would materialize there before him in his old-fashioned flannel pants, drawing back his racket in the same anticipatory way and then with a little, barely perceptible sigh—his arm still outstretched behind him—doubling over toward the ground, a quick, ugly rolling motion as though the racket were swinging *him*. The memory of it would make Richard pause, wondering if he was

48   pushing himself too hard. . . . The ball skipped by him for a point.

"Game!" Jack yelled.

But he could use it to advantage, too. Later, charging the net, he would remember the last point of his fourth all-island championship. He would yell and swing at the ball with all his might, slamming it to the court just as he had on the winning shot fourteen years ago. Back and forth across the court, propelled by these inexplicable surges and hesitations no one else could understand.

"Out!"

"Come on, June. Bear down!"

"Bear down yourself," she said snottily, but even so, they won the next three games.

The sun had gotten around the pine trees now and everyone was sweating. Richard's serve was giving Jack all kinds of trouble—June was winning points with backhands up the middle. He remembered Barbara Wright, the first girl he had ever gone out with. She used to hit them like that, with both hands, giggling on those rare occasions when the ball crossed the net. She always loudly insisted to anyone who would listen that what she really liked doing was waterskiing. Long after she had left him for someone else he'd catch sight of her on the sea far below, swinging back and forth over the water in her black bathing suit, very distant, very cool, her hair streaming out behind her as she crisscrossed the motorboat's wake. He used to wonder if she picked that time and place because she knew he'd be up there watching. He would always lose a point or two until he managed to put her out of his mind.

"Come on!" June yelled. "Bear down!"

It was a long rally this time. Sue had improved tremendously since July, and Jack had discovered the spot near the sideline where Richard always slowed down. The set was even at three.

"Had enough, Dicky?"

"Serve it!"

In order to give him a chance to play net, June started taking all the long shots landing in the middle. Richard was nervous about this; he felt vulnerable giving her responsibility for so much of the court. But at least he could concentrate on his forehand that way and they took the next two games without losing a point.

On one rally he slipped and fell near the left side of the net—the same spot where, on a rainy July afternoon the summer he was seventeen, he lost his virginity to Shannon Bathelder, the youngest of three sisters all of whom he was in love with at one time or another. They had decided to play despite the rain. He remembered the way her dress looked when it was soaked through, the way he had to keep swinging his racket back and forth in front of his shorts to hide his embarrassment. In running for the ball she had slipped and fallen near the net, calling him over to help her up. But she hadn't wanted to get up. She suddenly grabbed him and pulled him down on top of her breasts, pushing her tongue into his mouth and rolling him violently over on the clay. After that they had never played again. . . . He would see her on other courts with older men and be tormented by the thought that she was plotting the same accidental slip with them.

"Set!"

"We'll get you this time, hacker!"

The children had found their way up from the beach now—they waved their towels back and forth whenever Mommy won a point. Bobby and his friends were drifting over from the patio with the leftover beer. Every time Jack looked like he was getting tired one of them would run up to him with another can, ducking along the net like a ball boy retrieving strays.

The game went on.

"Out!" Jack yelled, at the top of his voice.

"Are you sure?"

"By a foot."

50   "Well, call them right away for God's sake!"

He remembered Kathy Lemp sitting there in the shade sipping root beer. Kathy Lemp who was delicate and who was supposedly going blind. She always insisted she was happy just watching. He used to go over between games to make sure she was comfortable; later he found out she told someone the real reason she split up with him was because of the ugly way his knees cracked when he ran.

"Good one, Richard Uncle Richard!"

"Atta serve, Richard baby!"

But Jack and Sue were on top of them now, pressing them back against the baseline where they couldn't do much with the ball. In a fit of anger Richard slammed a loose one over the fence. The kids disappeared down the cliff after it, shouting to each other about the shark.

On the next rally he and June converged on a lazy ball up the middle. They glanced at each other the way partners who haven't played with each other before will. Instantly he saw it was up to him to hit it. Just as he did so, just as he lined it up, she whispered something very low and soft in his ear.

"I want the name."

And he was so startled he missed the ball completely.

"Good shot, Dicky!"

"Game!"

"Hey, bear down Richard!" June said, loud enough so everyone could hear her this time. She walked back to the net as though nothing had happened.

After a while it became a pattern. Jack would try to split them apart with a soft one . . . the two of them would converge on it . . . June would look at him, he would look at her . . . she would whisper the same four words, just at the moment when he decided the ball was his.

"I want the name!"

"Strike three, Dicky!"

"Come on, Richard! The idea's to hit the damn ball!"

And eventually he had to change his strategy, staying by the net on those shots and letting June go back to them by herself.

"Break time!"

They wiped their faces on the beach towels the kids had left behind. Bobby took the opportunity to make a pyramid out of empty beer cans. Laurie and her boyfriend strolled off hand in hand toward the house.

"Let's go! Time to start!"

"It's not time yet!" Sue yelled. "I mean, I'm not fully recovered yet!"

They agreed to wait until the kids came back with the loose balls. As Richard stood there mopping his forehead he thought of Betty Schroeder wiping her face in the same deliberate way, starting first with the thin cross of perspiration that used to collect above the rim of her glasses, then working down over her face to another line of dampness that rested above the bodice of her tennis dress like a necklace. Long after it was time to start up again she would be rooted there with the towel pressed against her temples, standing so motionless it seemed she must have suffered some sort of attack and was holding the towel that way to relieve the pain.

Betty Schroeder. Big floppy hats over short red hair. The nicest laugh of any girl he ever knew. Betty Schroeder who drowned swimming by herself the night before he was going to take her to the club's summer dance.

"Richard?"

"No."

"But you'll never use it!"

"For God's sake, not now! Can't we talk about it later? Listen. What are we going to do about those soft ones up the middle? That's what's killing us. If I have to listen to that bastard Jack crow all night about beating us . . ."

"Nothing," she said airily.

52   "What do you mean nothing?"

"Nothing, that's all," and she sauntered back to the court with the maddening little strut she had when she was deliberately being mean.

The third set went badly right from the start. Jack's shots up the middle scored again and again. June couldn't be bothered chasing them. Sue was making all sorts of miraculous returns. His right leg was bothering him, the same leg he had injured twelve years before.

"Fault!"

"What are you talking about?"

"Fault! Call them yourself next time, Jack."

"It was good!"

"That was the third time this game, Jack! If you're not going to call them yourself then I'll have to. Simple as that!"

"Go on and play, Dicky!" they shouted from the sidelines. "It's only a game for Christ's sake!" Some of them started booing. When Richard walked back to the baseline to serve his face was bright red.

The second game, the game he played in his own imagination, was going badly, too. On one point he was apt to see three different girls—Mary Canning winding up, Suzy Thomas hitting, Lee Helms following through—a souped-up blur of breast, thigh, and arm that seemed to take up every available inch of the court, leaving him no room to maneuver. Cindy from the office had been miserably out of place the whole weekend, locking herself in the bathroom to cry. He'd invited Pam the last moment out of desperation and she had spent the entire two days trying to seduce Bobby. Sandra Wallace, June's idea, hadn't even known how to hold a racket, and talked of nothing except the difficulty she had getting appointments with her gynecologist.

"I want that name!" June whispered, over and over again. It was all he could hear now. Running back to cover for her, in the act of serving. "I want that name!"

His leg was really bothering him—it was all he could do just to get to the ball. Far out to sea a black cloud had formed across the sun. It hung there for a game, then moved in closer, as if coming in to watch.

"Let's go Uncle Jack and Aunt Sue!" the kids chanted, changing sides with no scruples now that it was apparent their mother's side was about to lose. "Let's go Uncle Jack and Aunt Sue!"

Richard stood it for as long as he could.

"Will you damn kids shut up!"

Everyone booed this time. One of Bobby's friends threw a beer can out on the court near his feet. He kicked it back and they booed even more. Bright red, looking like his life depended on it, he lost his serve.

"Game!"

"Let's go Uncle Jack and Aunt Sue!" the kids screamed defiantly, sensing the end was near.

But the sun was low enough to be in their eyes now. Jack was showing the effects of the beer. Slowly the momentum swung back—Richard and June rallied to within a game.

But now, just when they seemed to have them, June started acting strange. She was dropping back for the soft shots, getting there in plenty of time, suddenly stopping, not bothering to even try to hit it, letting the ball drop a foot within the baseline for a point.

"Sorry," she said the first time.

"For God's sake, June! Your ball!"

"Sorry!"

The sky was turning red. He was trying to rid himself of the second game now, trying to concentrate all his energy on the game he was playing right there, right now. He rolled back his shoulders, he stretched out his left arm to establish the ball in the air, he swung hard and followed through toward his toes. He did all the things he was supposed to do but all he could think about was Elaine standing there on the side of the court watching the

54   sunset with her mouth open at the beauty of it, his arm around her waist, her head coming down against his shoulder.

"One more! One more!" Jack yelled, pressing closer and closer to the net.

Elaine was the only one who ever mattered to him. Elaine he could remember down to the slightest detail—the mole on her left arm, the drinks she liked, her birthday . . .

"Fault!"

"Just play, dammit!"

"The name, Richard! The name!"

The two of them were perfectly teamed. He would run to the net for a ball and she would drop back instantly to cover, the two of them instinctively covering each other's weaknesses just as they complemented each other's strengths. She had a tremendous backhand—he had never seen a backhand that beautiful before— a yearning little sweep of the arm toward the sea like someone casting wheat. They would lie on the beach at night and talk about the game point by point. She would lean over him and kiss his eyes, first the right one, then the left, calming him down until who won no longer seemed important and all that mattered was being next to each other on the sand.

"Match point!" Jack yelled, throwing his fist into the air.

When it was his turn to serve she would stand there by the net and give a little involuntary twitch with her hips just before he hit the ball. One pretty little bump, one pretty little grind. She always wore sexy tennis outfits with lace panties. He found it very distracting and several times had asked her to stop. But for some reason she *couldn't* stop. She would try standing up straighter, she would even turn around and face him so her hips wouldn't show, but every time he wound up to serve she would make the same distracting twitch, as though it were a hiccup, a nervous reaction she couldn't control.

He finally yelled at her—she had run off in tears. For the first time in his life he abandoned a game before it was through, running after her until he caught up with her on the beach. He wiped her tears away, he asked her to marry him, deciding right there in the middle of their crying and laughing on the date, the guest list, and the names of their first son and daughter.

"Stop it!"

"Stop what?"

"I said stop it, bitch!"

The two games were merging now and he couldn't tell which was which. The weekend following their engagement she had twitched again before he served, just like the last time. Just like the last time, he yelled at her. He hadn't wanted to. He remembered telling himself she was as beautiful and good a woman as he'd ever find, that he was a madman to lose his temper over something so silly, that tennis was after all just a game. He hadn't wanted to scream at her but he did anyway, losing control of himself in front of everyone, using all the filthy names he could think of.

"Match point!"

June barely got to Sue's serve but passed Jack running in toward the net. She had taken the next ferry home. "Mommy!" the kids screamed. He had gotten his ring back in the mail. At deuce Sue double faulted. Three months later she had married a real estate broker in Connecticut. It would have been their match except June let another soft one deliberately drop in front of her. She had a baby boy. . . . He could see what June was doing now, trying to force him back to her so she could whisper in his ear.

"I want that name!"

"Bitch!"

"Match point!"

But he had no choice now . . . the summers, the girls he had known . . . everything about his life seemed to be coming down to that one point there in the late afternoon.

"I've got it!" he yelled.

The shot flew high and deep toward the baseline where Uncle Richard had died. In soaring so high, up against the sunset, it seemed to leave the game they were playing and enter the timeless one that was Richard's own. It was a very soft shot—it was headed down the middle of the court between them.

"I've got it!"

They converged. He was ready to hit it when another cramp, this one in his stomach, doubled him over and threw him helplessly to the ground. To those watching it seemed as though he had been flung there by an invisible, disdainful hand.

"Take it!" he screamed, dropping his racket in pain.

She looked at him. For a moment it seemed she would let the ball drop there by his feet without trying for it. For that one questioning moment, as the shot bounced out of his past and into her future, their eyes met and they both understood.

"Yes!" he screamed. "Yours! Take it!"

She drew her racket back. She hit a gentle lob that seemed to stay in the air forever. . . . Up, up, up. . . . Poised there at the apogee like a star shell about to burst. . . . Poised there as if admiring the view, choosing its landing place down below. . . . Down, down, down. . . . Jack and Sue taken by surprise, running frantically back to cover, the crowd on the sideline rising to their feet. . . . Down, down, down. . . . The sun touching the water, his whole life seeming to rush by him in a blur. . . . Down . . . down . . . down. . . .

"Out!" Jack yelled.

And in the last second the lob had before rolling exhausted to a stop it saw June smile. It saw June pat her stomach in satisfaction and smile a secret smile to the Richard who was yet to be.

The Bass, the River, and Sheila Mant

THERE was a summer in my life when the only creature that seemed lovelier to me than a largemouth bass was Sheila Mant. I was fourteen. The Mants had rented the cottage next to ours on the river; with their parties, their frantic games of softball, their constant comings and goings, they appeared to me denizens of a brilliant existence. "Too noisy by half," my mother quickly decided, but I would have given anything to be invited to one of their parties, and when my parents went to bed I would sneak through the woods to their hedge and stare enchanted at the candlelit swirl of white dresses and bright, paisley skirts.

Sheila was the middle daughter—at seventeen, all but out of reach. She would spend her days sunbathing on a float my Uncle Sierbert had moored in their cove, and before July was over I had learned all her moods. If she lay flat on the diving board with her hand trailing idly in the water, she was pensive, not to be disturbed. On her side, her head propped up by her arm, she was observant, considering those around her with a look that seemed queenly and severe. Sitting up, arms tucked around her long, suntanned legs, she was approachable, but barely, and it was only in those glorious moments when she stretched herself prior to entering the water that her various suitors found the courage to come near.

These were many. The Dartmouth heavyweight crew would

scull by her house on their way upriver, and I think all eight of them must have been in love with her at various times during the summer; the coxswain would curse at them through his megaphone, but without effect—there was always a pause in their pace when they passed Sheila's float. I suppose to these jaded twenty-year-olds she seemed the incarnation of innocence and youth, while to me she appeared unutterably suave, the epitome of sophistication. I was on the swim team at school, and to win her attention would do endless laps between my house and the Vermont shore, hoping she would notice the beauty of my flutter kick, the power of my crawl. Finishing, I would boost myself up onto our dock and glance casually over toward her, but she was never watching, and the miraculous day she was, I immediately climbed the diving board and did my best tuck and a half for her, and continued diving until she had left and the sun went down and my longing was like a madness and I couldn't stop.

It was late August by the time I got up the nerve to ask her out. The tortured will-I's, won't-I's, the agonized indecision over what to say, the false starts toward her house and embarrassed retreats—the details of these have been seared from my memory, and the only part I remember clearly is emerging from the woods toward dusk while they were playing softball on their lawn, as bashful and frightened as a unicorn.

Sheila was stationed halfway between first and second, well outside the infield. She didn't seem surprised to see me—as a matter of fact, she didn't seem to see me at all.

"If you're playing second base, you should move closer," I said.

She turned—I took the full brunt of her long red hair and well-spaced freckles.

"I'm playing outfield," she said, "I don't like the responsibility of having a base."

"Yeah, I can understand that," I said, though I couldn't. "There's a band in Dixford tomorrow night at nine. Want to go?"

One of her brothers sent the ball sailing over the leftfielder's
head; she stood and watched it disappear toward the river.

"You have a car?" she said, without looking up.

I played my master stroke. "We'll go by canoe."

I spent all of the following day polishing it. I turned it upside
down on our lawn and rubbed every inch with Brillo, hosing off
the dirt, wiping it with chamois until it gleamed as bright as alumi-
num ever gleamed. About five, I slid it into the water, arranging
cushions near the bow so Sheila could lean on them if she was in
one of her pensive moods, propping up my father's transistor
radio by the middle thwart so we could have music when we came
back. Automatically, without thinking about it, I mounted my
Mitchell reel on my Pfleuger spinning rod and stuck it in the stern.

I say automatically, because I never went anywhere that summer without a fishing rod. When I wasn't swimming laps to
impress Sheila, I was back in our driveway practicing casts, and
when I wasn't practicing casts, I was tying the line to Tosca, our
springer spaniel, to test the reel's drag, and when I wasn't doing
any of those things, I was fishing the river for bass.

Too nervous to sit at home, I got in the canoe early and started
paddling in a huge circle that would get me to Sheila's dock
around eight. As automatically as I brought along my rod, I tied
on a big Rapala plug, let it down into the water, let out some line
and immediately forgot all about it.

It was already dark by the time I glided up to the Mants' dock.
Even by day the river was quiet, most of the summer people
preferring Sunapee or one of the other nearby lakes, and at night
it was a solitude difficult to believe, a corridor of hidden life that
ran between banks like a tunnel. Even the stars were part of it.
They weren't as sharp anywhere else; they seemed to have chosen
the river as a guide on their slow wheel toward morning, and in
the course of the summer's fishing, I had learned all their names.

I was there ten minutes before Sheila appeared. I heard the slam of their screen door first, then saw her in the spotlight as she came slowly down the path. As beautiful as she was on the float, she was even lovelier now—her white dress went perfectly with her hair, and complimented her figure even more than her swimsuit.

It was her face that bothered me. It had on its delightful fullness a very dubious expression.

"Look," she said. "I can get Dad's car."

"It's faster this way," I lied. "Parking's tense up there. Hey, it's safe. I won't tip it or anything."

She let herself down reluctantly into the bow. I was glad she wasn't facing me. When her eyes were on me, I felt like diving in the river again from agony and joy.

I pried the canoe away from the dock and started paddling upstream. There was an extra paddle in the bow, but Sheila made no move to pick it up. She took her shoes off, and dangled her feet over the side.

Ten minutes went by.

"What kind of band?" she said.

"It's sort of like folk music. You'll like it."

"Eric Caswell's going to be there. He strokes number four."

"No kidding?" I said. I had no idea who she meant.

"What's that sound?" she said, pointing toward shore.

"Bass. That splashing sound?"

"Over there."

"Yeah, bass. They come into the shallows at night to chase frogs and moths and things. Big largemouths. *Micropetrus salmonides*," I added, showing off.

"I think fishing's dumb," she said, making a face. "I mean, it's boring and all. Definitely dumb."

Now I have spent a great deal of time in the years since wondering why Sheila Mant should come down so hard on fishing. Was her father a fisherman? Her antipathy toward fishing nothing more than normal filial rebellion? Had she tried it once? A messy encounter with worms? It doesn't matter. What does, is that at that fragile moment in time I would have given anything not to appear dumb in Sheila's severe and unforgiving eyes.

She hadn't seen my equipment yet. What I *should* have done, of course, was push the canoe in closer to shore and carefully slide the rod into some branches where I could pick it up again in the morning. Failing that, I could have surreptitiously dumped the whole outfit overboard, written off the forty or so dollars as love's tribute. What I actually *did* do was gently lean forward, and slowly, ever so slowly, push the rod back through my legs toward the stern where it would be less conspicuous.

It must have been just exactly what the bass was waiting for. Fish will trail a lure sometimes, trying to make up their mind whether or not to attack, and the slight pause in the plug's speed caused by my adjustment was tantalizing enough to overcome the bass's inhibitions. My rod, safely out of sight at last, bent double. The line, tightly coiled, peeled off the spool with the shrill, tearing zip of a high-speed drill.

Four things occurred to me at once. One, that it was a bass. Two, that it was a big bass. Three, that it was the biggest bass I had ever hooked. Four, that Sheila Mant must not know.

"What was that?" she said, turning half around.

"Uh, what was what?"

"That buzzing noise."

"Bats."

She shuddered, quickly drew her feet back into the canoe. Every instinct I had told me to pick up the rod and strike back at the bass, but there was no need to—it was already solidly hooked. Downstream, an awesome distance downstream, it jumped clear of the water, landing with a concussion heavy enough to ripple the entire river. For a moment, I thought it was gone, but then the rod was bending again, the tip dancing into the water. Slowly, not making any motion that might alert Sheila, I reached down to tighten the drag.

While all this was going on, Sheila had begun talking and it was a few minutes before I was able to catch up with her train of thought.

"I went to a party there. These fraternity men. Katherine says I could get in there if I wanted. I'm thinking more of UVM or Bennington. Somewhere I can ski."

The bass was slanting toward the rocks on the New Hampshire side by the ruins of Donaldson's boathouse. It had to be an old bass—a young one probably wouldn't have known the rocks were there. I brought the canoe back out into the middle of the river, hoping to head it off.

"That's neat," I mumbled. "Skiing. Yeah, I can see that."

"Eric said I have the figure to model, but I thought I should get an education first. I mean, it might be a while before I get started and all. I was thinking of getting my hair styled, more swept back? I mean, Ann-Margret? Like hers, only shorter."

She hesitated. "Are we going backwards?"

We were. I had managed to keep the bass in the middle of the river away from the rocks, but it had plenty of room there, and for the first time a chance to exert its full strength. I quickly computed the weight necessary to draw a fully loaded canoe backwards—the thought of it made me feel faint.

"It's just the current," I said hoarsely. "No sweat or anything."

I dug in deeper with my paddle. Reassured, Sheila began talking about something else, but all my attention was taken up now with the fish. I could feel its desperation as the water grew shallower. I could sense the extra strain on the line, the frantic way it cut back and forth in the water. I could visualize what it looked like—the gape of its mouth, the flared gills and thick, vertical tail. The bass couldn't have encountered many forces in its long life that it wasn't capable of handling, and the unrelenting tug at its mouth must have been a source of great puzzlement and mounting panic.

Me, I had problems of my own. To get to Dixford, I had to

paddle up a sluggish stream that came into the river beneath a covered bridge. There was a shallow sandbar at the mouth of this stream—weeds on one side, rocks on the other. Without doubt, this is where I would lose the fish.

"I have to be careful with my complexion. I tan, but in segments. I can't figure out if it's even worth it. I wouldn't even do it probably. I saw Jackie Kennedy in Boston and she wasn't tan at all."

Taking a deep breath, I paddled as hard as I could for the middle, deepest part of the bar. I could have threaded the eye of a needle with the canoe, but the pull on the stern threw me off and I overcompensated—the canoe veered left and scraped bottom. I pushed the paddle down and shoved. A moment of hesitation . . . a moment more. . . . The canoe shot clear into the deeper water of the stream. I immediately looked down at the rod. It was bent in the same, tight arc—miraculously, the bass was still on.

The moon was out now. It was low and full enough that its beam shone directly on Sheila there ahead of me in the canoe, washing her in a creamy, luminous glow. I could see the lithe, easy shape of her figure. I could see the way her hair curled down off her shoulders, the proud, alert tilt of her head, and all these things were as a tug on my heart. Not just Sheila, but the aura she carried about her of parties and casual touchings and grace. Behind me, I could feel the strain of the bass, steadier now, growing weaker, and this was another tug on my heart, not just the bass but the beat of the river and the slant of the stars and the smell of the night, until finally it seemed I would be torn apart between longings, split in half. Twenty yards ahead of us was the road, and once I pulled the canoe up on shore, the bass would be gone, irretrievably gone. If instead I stood up, grabbed the rod and started pumping, I would have it—as tired as the bass was, there was no chance it could get away. I reached down for the rod, hesitated, looked up to where Sheila was stretching herself lazily

64   toward the sky, her small breasts rising beneath the soft fabric of her dress, and the tug was too much for me, and quicker than it takes to write down, I pulled a penknife from my pocket and cut the line in half.

With a sick, nauseous feeling in my stomach, I saw the rod unbend.

"My legs are sore," Sheila whined. "Are we there yet?"

Through a superhuman effort of self-control, I was able to beach the canoe and help Sheila off. The rest of the night is much foggier. We walked to the fair—there was the smell of popcorn, the sound of guitars. I may have danced once or twice with her, but all I really remember is her coming over to me once the music was done to explain that she would be going home in Eric Caswell's Corvette.

"Okay," I mumbled.

For the first time that night she looked at me, really looked at me.

"You're a funny kid, you know that?"

Funny. Different. Dreamy. Odd. How many times was I to hear that in the years to come, all spoken with the same quizzical, half-accusatory tone Sheila used then. Poor Sheila! Before the month was over, the spell she cast over me was gone, but the memory of that lost bass haunted me all summer and haunts me still. There would be other Sheila Mants in my life, other fish, and though I came close once or twice, it was these secret, hidden tuggings in the night that claimed me, and I never made the same mistake again.

Nickel a Throw

THESE are the things Gooden sees from his perch eight feet above the dunking tub at the Dixford Congregational Church's Charity bazaar.

The sun touching the ridge on the river's western shore. Orange, underlining of black.

The river itself. A canoe. A boy in a canoe lighting sparklers.

A ferris wheel turning slowly clockwise, dipping into the people massed at its base.

Strings of light. Lights as aural as sounds. Red snap, yellow crackle, blue pop.

Refreshment stands. A tent on the town common. Lobsters held by the belly. Faces disappearing into wads of cotton candy, emerging pink.

Individuals. A girl climbing a slanting rope ladder over an inflated cushion. A baby squatting behind a dusty-looking golden retriever, pulling out tufts of the dog's hair. The town band badly tuned. Professorial-looking types from the college, in cardigans, in July. Summer campers down from the mountain, roped together. Stuffed E.T.'s dragged by the ears. Farmers, bald. Farmers' wives, shy-looking, toting bags. Ray Stanton in a straw hat manning the goldfish booth. Gooden's wife Angela dispensing change behind the baked goods, smiling with a radiance that pleased and puzzled him at the same time. Angela in the blue gingham dress she had worn on their first date seventeen years ago, as beautiful and desirable as she had been then.

A Frisbee appearing from nowhere. Hovering. Observing. Sailing away.

Space. Starlight. Shadows. And then much closer, in the narrow chute left between the tub and the booth's entrance, a teenager with purple streaks in his hair cocking back his arm to hurl a tennis ball at the saucer-sized target beneath Gooden's stool.

"Missed," Gooden says timidly, in a voice hardly above a whisper.

The boy doesn't pay for another ball. Gooden sees how long the lines are at the other booths, sees how short it is for his, remembers Stanton's advice about banter.

"You throw like a girl," he says, a bit louder.

The boy struts away. Gooden sees the razor blades hanging from his ears, sees the yellow hair mixed in with the purple, hears the music from his huge transistor, tries to remember the right name for it.

"Runts!" he yells, too late. The boy is gone.

Five minutes go by before another customer arrives. Gooden sits on the stool with his head in his hands like Quasimodo above the gargoyles, worried. He sees Angela slicing bread. The sight of her—wanting to please her—shoots through him in a surge that almost makes him jump into the tub from joy.

A ball whizzes by his head. Down below, a foul-looking man with a size eighteen neck winds up again.

"Shit," he hisses, as the ball curves wide.

He slaps down a nickel, picks up another ball. His throwing is stiff and brutal. Ball mashed between fingers, brought up like a sledge hammer, punched more than thrown.

"Missed!" Gooden yells.

The man's friends begin to ride him. Tubucular-looking with

slicked-back hair, "Elvis Lives" buttons, Budweisers stuck in their
pants like guns.

"Cretins!" Gooden yells, in a high-pitched voice so different
from his usual modulation that it startles even him.

He senses their hostility but for once in his life it doesn't
frighten him. Hostility brings in the nickels. Hostility makes the
booth a success, enriches the bazaar, supports charities, feeds
babies, does good.

"What's the matter, moron? Be a sport and try again."

His loafers. His wire-rimmed glasses and neat sports coat. His
superior height there on the stool. Gooden can tell each of these
things infuriates the man, but his words anger him not, and the
balls fly at him with diminished force. Gooden searches the beefy
face for clues.

"Drunkard!" he shouts, slapping the stool's side to gain his
attention. "Inebriate!"

He hurls all the insults he can think of, as if they are balls he is
firing back at him, aiming for the spot in him that is his trigger.
Redneck, hick, bum. But none of them connect, and the man is
shaking his head with a laugh, and proudly patting his stomach,
and turning away with his friends to the next booth.

The mashed ball. The axlike chop of the arm. The violent, satisfied grunt as he lets it go. Gooden remembers these things and
then suddenly he has it, and it is as clear and bright and certain as
the lights on the ferris wheel's base.

"Wife beater!" he screams.

The man stops. The man wheels slowly around and comes back
to the booth, minus his friends. He takes a nickel out of his
pocket, places it on the felt matting beside the bucket of balls. He's
a long time in selecting one, but when he does, he closes and
recloses his hand over it, throttling its air. He advances to the line
chalked in the grass twenty feet from the tub. He stares toward

the target with a grimness and concentration that are totally differ-ent from the casual malice he had shown before. In the spotlight, in the tunnel of visiblity left between them, it is he and Gooden alone.

"You beat her with your hands," Gooden says softly, almost cooing. "You beat her because it makes you feel good. It makes you feel like a man. You do it until she begs you to stop, and when she begs, you slap her again."

The man brings his hand up to his eyes as if the light is blinding him, but then Gooden realizes it isn't the light, but that he is throwing the ball—that the fuzzy, moon-sized object advancing toward him is the tennis ball released from his hand. "Missed!" he says to himself, with a rush of exhilaration, but the ball strikes the center of the target, tripping the spring that holds him suspended, and the moment he realizes this, he is on his way down.

"I must prepare myself for this," he thinks, but before he decides how, he is at the bottom of the tub in a cloud of bubbles that pop apart on his nose. There is no shock involved. The water feels cool, but yielding. The geyser of spray shooting up from the tub, the man's triumphant yell—he is aware of neither. The tub is soundless. Above him, the surface is dappled with everchanging shapes and colors, like a kaleidoscope. As he shimmies toward it, the water rides his shirt up his chest with the same gentle, teasing tug Angela would use in slipping off his clothes.

When he emerges gasping at the surface there is a crowd wait-ing in line for balls. Holding his fist above his head like a vic-torious prizefighter, Gooden climbs the ladder to his stool.

He goes back to the things he has sensed before, checking his emotions the way another man would check his bones. His booth's line is as long as the other lines: envy gone. Angela above a tray of cupcakes: love intact. The view: loftier now, embracing not only the ferris wheel and the ring of lights and the river, but the valley in which the river flowed, the dark mass of hill on either side, the frame in which the fair is mounted.

Damp, his clothes wrapped on him like wet papier-mâché, he turns his attention to the balls which fly in more rapid procession past his head.

Teenagers mostly. Petty thieves, masturbators, nickelless liars— he doesn't waste his time on these. It's the next one in line that interests him. A tall, supercilious man with a complexion like cheap corduroy.

"Wimp!" Gooden yells, watching his reaction.

With the man is a girl half his age who strokes the back of his blazer as he throws. He throws studiously, juggling the ball in his hand as if weighing it, squinting, flipping it with a halfhearted gesture that seems to indicate he wants it back.

"Professor!" Gooden shouts.

Almost too easy. The man takes a step forward and smiles, as if he has been called upon to bow.

"Humanist!"

A touch of uncertainty in the smile.

"Sophist!"

A frown. The professor looks around to see if anyone can hear. Bored, the girl tries to pull him away, but he shrugs her off, takes a nickel out of his pocket—takes out three. He cradles the balls in the crook of his arm, like snowballs.

"You sit there in class mumbling inanities," Gooden says as the professor winds up. "You serve up beauty and truth on a tray to morons who will never have any use for either. You prepare dolts to be assistant managers at MacDonald's, and in the depths of your soul you know you're as banal as they are."

Until now, the professor has managed to keep an aloof, mildly amused look on his face. "Second-rater!" Gooden yells, and with that the nap of the corduroy becomes tighter; he grabs the ball as

70   violently as the wife beater and throws it with all his might toward the stool.

"You're superfluous," Gooden whispers. "A relic. A traitor to the truth."

Gooden keeps talking as the ball sails closer, speaking more to it than to the professor, as if his words are a guidance system that automatically corrects variations in its flight. Time-server, dilettante, bore. The words find the ball and draw it with a cymballike concussion against the target's metal plate.

A bellywop this time. A gusher of spray breaking apart at its apogee, drenching the people at the next booth. The pain slaps him over in a tight somersault; his head brushes the wooden side of the tub on his way down. He notices things he missed the first time in. How the tub is greasy with vegetation, as if the water hadn't been changed since last year's fair. How dark and oily the water is. How by curling his legs under him he can not only cushion his landing against the bottom, but use it as a springboard to shoot back to the surface, emerging as straight and spectacularly as a submarine-launched missile.

The crowd screams from delight.

"Thank you," Gooden yells, mounting the ladder. "Thank you very much!"

A man in his thirties dressed in jeans and a red checkered shirt separates himself from the mass of bodies waiting in line. One sleeve is empty, and there are lines on his face that belie the youthfulness of his smile. Gooden has seen him around town working at a variety of jobs, all of them menial. He reaches for a name—Bob, Mike, something simple. Whatever it is, he throws with endearing formality. Sideways, peeking over his stub of a shoulder like a pitcher checking the runner on first.

Gooden thinks: "No, not this one." But the power he feels is like a new sense and he feels compelled to test it the way a person

without touch, regaining it, would touch everything, even if it
meant burns.

"Drunk driver," Gooden says, probing. "You were drunk, you killed a kid, and your missing arm can't make up for the guilt I see on your face."

The young man looks at him uncomprehendingly—he stops in midstride, balking. Gooden tries again.

"Dealer in drugs. Pothead. Junkie."

Gooden tries to look harder, not at the man himself, but the larger frame surrounding the man, the frame he had only become conscious of when he first mounted the stool. He sees the man and the other innocent, foolish, armless men his age of which he is representative, and then he has it, and it comes out sadly and reluctantly, nothing personal, with no wish to blame only him.

"Nam," he says simply. "Nam."

Bob or Mike or Bill takes out a dollar, and with one hand scoops up balls from the table on which they are arranged. He no longer throws like Whitey Ford. He lobs them overhand like grenades, as reluctantly as Gooden says the word, but with the same kind of compulsion.

The two of them in spotlight. Balls in a rainbow arc. Closer, closer . . .

"Nam!" Gooden yells, and the ball embeds itself in the target, ejecting him into the air. Feet kicking, arms flailing, mouth open, he falls against the metal rim of the tub and backflips over, his arm scratching open on a nail someone has forgotten to remove from the side. As he floats to the surface, a watery spiral of blood climbs with him. He fights down a panicky urge to inhale.

It takes longer to mount the ladder. Climbing, he thinks of Stanton asking him to volunteer.

Stanton (smiling): "It's a funny job."

Gooden (curious): "Funny how?"

Stanton (mysterious): "It changes a man being up there."
Gooden (worried): "Changes how?"
Stanton (laughing): "You'll see."

He can pick Stanton out now, grounded among the goldfish and the ping-pong balls, twirling a cane. Gooden wants to call out to him, tell him that he is right. He does feel changed, feels like he does when he's finished his monthly bottle of wine and the trivialities that beset him have fled. The stool seems much higher than before, as if there is a handle on its bottom and someone is cranking him up. Not only does he see the frame of mountains ringing the fair, but the plains forming the inverted wall on which the frame hangs, plains sparkled with lights and mysterious undulations.

A ball heads toward his face. He bats it away with contemptuous, pawlike gesture—a boy brushing aside flies.

Higher. The varicolored lights of the midway become streamers radiating out of the Maypole on top of which he sits. He shivers, hugs himself in the thrill of it. It's much harder now to pick out faces at the other booths, and the only person beside Stanton he can identify for sure is Angela, looking up at him from the baked goods, her expression shorn of everything except question. Seeing her, he has the urge to show off—he quickly estimates his chances of doing a handstand on the stool—and he is about to call out to her to watch when he makes the mistake of looking down.

The tub is a thimble. A shot glass. A target through a bombsight. He stares at it in a kind of vertigo—he has to grab the stool with both hands to keep from falling off.

"Steady, Gooden," he says, closing his eyes.

Below him, a mass of swirling shapes.

"Fornicators!" Gooden shouts, deepening his voice like a king calling to his subjects from a throne. "Vainglorious egotists!"

A nickel a throw. Spake Rollins, president of Dixford's hospital,

clothed in flannel as soft and fine as a girl's hair. Smiler, shaker of   73
hands, a born politician throwing out the first pitch.

"You feed on other people's suffering," Gooden shouts. "You have taken pain and turned it into a raw material to enrich a handful of doctors and administrators, doing it so smoothly and secretly that people call you humanitarians and you bask in that glow."

The ball striking home, Gooden spreading his arms out like a sky-diver, steering himself for the thimble. . . .

A nickel a throw. Sylvia Thorpe, architect, her current lover dropping balls into her hand as delicately as grapes.

"Builder of malls!" Gooden shouts, like a town crier warning of plague. "Designer of prisons, destroyer of grace!"

The head-first entry. The concussion on his face; the water tumbling him over and over, drowning him, not permitting him to drown. . . .

Nickel a throw. Helmut Konner, owner of the mill, Gooden's boss. Taut, handsome, pulling his wife through the obsequious faces waiting in line as if she is a prize he has won at an earlier booth. On his head, every hair stays obediently in place; on his face, each wrinkle lies dormant. He picks up the ball like a belonging—an expensive paperweight, precious china, a deed.

"Konner!" Gooden yells, as if the name is accusation enough. "Poisoner of the river, poisoner of the air! You fired Henry Waite because he suggested putting in pollution controls on stack number five. You bribed the state inspector so he wouldn't report what comes out of that discharge pipe near the elementary school. You lay off the mill hands after nineteen weeks so they'll never be eligible for unemployment and call it their 'vacation'—give them the minimum wage and moan about how they're cheating you. You make your furniture out of the cheapest wood and charge the highest prices, your ethics being the only thing shoddier than your products."

74   On the bottom now, gathering his legs under him for the thrust back to the surface. But the power in his legs is gone, the water presses the buoyancy out of him like a piston, and he begins to gag. Urine! he wants to shout. Sewage! Filth! He sees bits of fabric stuck on the tub's sides, senses other people who have been dunked in previous fairs, tries to summon strength from them as he endures the slow, exhausting rise to the top.

"Thank you," he yells weakly, draping himself on the ladder. "Thank you very much."

He climbs wearily back to his stool. The line has grown since Konner. It stretches back beyond the goldfish booth, past the canning exhibit, past the ferris wheel, past the church, up Main Street toward the interstate highway where it forms a black strip on the lighter gray. Seeing it, a chill clutches at Gooden's middle, and he almost climbs down from his perch. Just in time he spots Angela, leaving her baked goods, edging her way toward him through the crowd.

His dizziness is worse. The long hours alone beneath the sun when no one came, the booth's sudden popularity, the series of falls—it's adding up. Down below people are fanning themselves with their programs, but the stool is so high that he's exposed to the buffets of a different air stream. Smells blow past. Familiar, carnival smells first: dough being fried, maple syrup, cheap perfume. They act as a stimulant to fainter, more distant smells: the stone-hard smell of—what? Appalachia? The gagging sweet smell of refineries around Pittsburgh; the smothered smell of mashed and cooking wheat further west. Bits of jetsam float by. A stalk of corn from—where? Iowa? It could be Iowa. It could be orange blossoms from California, sticky pine needles from the Pacific Northwest. They deposit themselves on his wet shirt as if it is a fly tape attracting the detritus of the entire continent—the soot and the ashes and the flowers.

He shivers so feverishly that his seeing becomes caught up with it, too, and his vision blurs and jumps frames and brings in not only the here and now, but the past as well. There is a stir in the line, and to the head steps his father, not as he had been when he had died, but as he would be now, nearly a hundred, shrunken and lame.

He examines the balls like they are eggs, holding them to the light, shaking them inquisitively by his ear. His father who from the day Gooden was born never stopped worrying that his boy might turn out to be smarter than he was and leave him behind. He rolls his sleeves up, brings his thick farmer's arms above his head so Gooden can see the knots and scars.

"This is truth," Gooden says, talking for him. "The truth is in my fingers and hands, the misery in my back, the stiffness in my knees. Truth is suffering and pain."

"Lies!" Gooden shouts, but his father has selected a ball now, and is throwing it at the target with surprising force. It sails wide, but another person joins him at the head of the line, and it is his mother, grown old now, too, in the soft gray dress they had buried her in fourteen years before. His mother who dreamed large dreams for him, and—making him share them—condemned him to failure. She picks up a ball, smiles her sweetest smile, closes her eyes.

"Truth is soft," Gooden says, reading her thoughts. "Things will get better. What will be will be. Everything works out for the best. Truth is something prettied up, a spoiled daughter dressed in fine clothes."

"Truth is neither hard nor soft!" Gooden shouts. "Truth is the trajectory between hearts! Truth is this stool, this target, this tub."

They shake their heads in the regretful, indulgent way of loving parents. His father puts his arms around his mother, guides her in the proper motion for throwing the ball, and Gooden is so busy trying to form the mingled exhilaration and despair he feels into words that he doesn't see that the ball is making directly for the target.

"Truth is love!" he wants to shout, but he is already plummeting

76 stonelike toward the tub. He knows what to expect now—the core-piercing coldness, the turgidness, the stench—but even so, it is worse than before, and he claws his way in panic back to the top.

The ladder sways. His feet and hands tremble. He fights down the urge to bite the rung.

His mother and father are still there, but before he can call out to them that he is okay, they are pushed away by frowning, officious-looking women in blue pants. After a pause, a squarish man in a general's uniform steps forward. Gooden is still wondering what a general could be doing in Dixford, when he begins to throw balls rapid-fire, not just at the target but everywhere, forcing everyone to duck. A second later he is joined by a man Gooden recognizes as president of one of the television networks—a bald, folksy man he's seen in commercials promoting the shows that will appear in the fall. He throws balls with as much gusto as the general, turning to say something to a functionary at his shoulder with a pad, the functionary nodding, laughing, as if they have stumbled upon a new game show that promises to be a hit.

Their balls come closer and closer to the target—the general's are illuminated by neon into tracers—when they both suddenly stop and stand respectfully aside, making way for President Reagan in a cardigan sweater and white bucks. He looks at the ball, looks at the crowd, points to himself, shrugs a question mark, laughs at their applause, picks the ball up, kisses it, poses, kisses it again, cocks it back over his ear like a football, poses, kisses it one last time, lets it go. As he follows through, his lips, visible only to Gooden, form the words "Screw you."

"Old man!" Gooden yells hoarsely. "Old man, old man, old man!"

There is no glory left in it anymore. If he manages to climb out of the tub a final time and mount the ladder, it is only from a kind of half-demented persistence so hopeless and irrational that it mocks itself. He just barely makes it back to the stool, but when he does, he stands on the seat and spreads his arms apart like someone preparing to swan dive. Miraculously, his shivering stops. He stares down at the crowd waiting to throw at him with something approaching calm.

Angela steps forward to the head of the line, the breeze teasing back the curls off her forehead, the light showing off her figure. Gooden waves to her, points to the nickels piled on the felt matting, indicates the crowd. He can't be sure, but she seems impressed. In the dark, in the flickering yellow beams, it could be admiration that is caught on her face. There is something definitely new there—not new, but something he hasn't seen in years. A radiance, a concentration and dreaminess combined, the look of a woman examining herself in a mirror and thinking of someone else at the same time. I love, I am loved, it seems to say. He waits for her to lift her eyes to the stool, so he can acknowledge her love and reflect it back, but she just stands there, and when he calls to her, she drops her eyes and holds them on the ground.

Gooden tries to force his vision away from her, but she stands in the beam where his compulsion must have her.

"Your love is not for me," he says softly, without malice. "I am an embarrassment to you, a spectacle. Those curls, that dress. Ornaments for a lover I don't know."

He teeters, and for a moment it seems that he will fall off the stool of his own volition. Catching himself, he stands erect on the stool again and leans his head back as far as it will go, a raven screaming to the sky.

"Cheater!" he yells, joyfully.

Her eyes meet his. He waits to see if she will pay for a ball, then sees one in her hand, realizes that she had already taken one before stepping out of line. She brings it over her head with the graceful, feminine gesture she would use in the shower, stretching up on tiptoes as he soaped her back. Turning toward him, she lets it go, as delicately and wistfully as a girl boosting a butterfly back into flight.

Gooden sees the ball leave her hand, sees her follow through as a lingering wave, then the ball hides her face and comes toward him in slow motion.

One part of him falls fast. The other half—the half that still sits on the stool watching the clown in him fall—drops slower, giving him time to see himself in all his shame: the fattest man in Dixford splashing into a tub of water as his neighbors cheer.

He hits bottom and starts toward the surface, but just as his head begins to break free, a hand comes down on it and forces him back under. He wiggles, tries to slip away and emerge more to the side, but another hand reaches in and holds him there, then another, then a third. In the blurred refraction of the lights he can see the wife beater and the professor and Sylvia Thorpe and Mr. Konner and then Angela, too, looking down at him with the stern, grotesque expressions of spectators at an aquarium, their arms the spokes of a wheel at the hub of which is his skull.

Finished, he thinks calmly. He closes his eyes and waits for the darkness to take him, but a moment before it does, the pressure on his head suddenly relaxes and he is permitted to bob belly-up to the top. Alive, gasping, whimpering, warned.

Why I Love America

THE station was better. All he needed there was a bag—the bag that had come home to him when Rufus Junior was killed—and the transit goons would leave him alone. "Going on Washington," he would mumble when they shook him awake. "Going on Baltimore, going on D.C." They were too stupid to ask for his ticket. He would watch them slouch across the waiting room toward the old men who had fallen asleep against the lockers, their nightsticks pressing against their bellies like hard brown dildos. "Assholes," he would whisper, spitting. By the time they started shoving them out toward the street, he was already asleep again. Eddie Dixon, Manassa Jones, Richie Brown. They were the kind of men who life had pushed around, but if they weren't smart enough to bring a bag, it was no concern of his.

It was harder at the library. Snipes, the guard at the entrance, always took his bag away before he let him in. "Morning, Mr. R.," he would say. "Not smuggling anything today, are you?" He would turn the bag over on the X-ray machine and shake it and give him a check so he could get it back when he left. Rufus didn't enjoy giving it up. It had Rufus Junior's initials on the side, and his army address was still on the tag, just where he had put it the day he had left. But bag or no bag, the principle was the same. In the station you pretended to travel; in the library you pretended to read.

The table was in the stacks, the metal ones where they kept the mildewed encyclopedias that smelled like bananas. There were three chairs around it, and they were always empty. The light was bad there; the stream from the air-conditioning flowed elsewhere. Beside the table was a square window the size of a porthole. Through it, he could just make out the rubble of the demolished train station, and the fine chalky dust that hovered over it like smoke. Between the station and the library was police headquarters—when he wasn't pretending to read, he would watch the cruisers pull up to the back door. A blur of motion, a faint metallic slam, and whoever they had fastened onto was hurried inside.

Rufus turned back to the book.

It didn't matter which one it was. He took them at random from the shelves, propping them open in the middle of the table where they would catch his head if he dozed. He wasn't interested in words. In the station, he had felt oppressed by the weight of people—people coming, people going, people waiting around— but it was nothing compared to the oppression he felt when he thought of all the words gathered there above him in the stacks. If you waited long enough, people moved and left you alone. Words never moved, and when he accidentally took down a book without illustrations, he would immediately slam the covers shut, as if to kill a spider he had spotted there on the page. They were someone else's words, not his. They had never been his, never would be his, never could be his, and all the time he sat there, he was conscious of them lying in wait at his back—an infinite army of meaningless black bugs waiting to be squished.

Even worse was Miss Brint.

He wasn't sure what her job was. Hushing kids, hassling old men—that was about it. She looked machine-tooled—he winced every time he saw her. Her hair was the color of tinsel, her breasts seemed as small and hard as thumbtacks, her legs reminded him of tweezers. Her voice didn't come out like a normal woman's; it crinkled out.

"How are you this glorious A.M.?" she would say, helping herself to one of the empty chairs. "You're looking very chipper and spry. It's like I was telling Mrs. Summers yesterday afternoon. It's so refreshing to find someone who actually likes to read. Those other men. Well, I don't know why they even come here in the first place. We're giving out books, not donuts. Speaking of which. I've brought you another one, Mr. R. It's a study of black civilization in West Africa by that man up at Harvard. The moment I saw it, I knew it was for you."

He was lucky if it was only one. Sometimes she put two or three books on the table, and once it had been an entire set: *American Slavery—Three Centuries of Despair*. She read the title for him that time; usually, he was left to figure out the subject for himself. The ones that had pictures in he would linger over, but with most he would simply turn each page until he came to the end, sliding it across the table toward the pile of those he had already turned through. Miss Brint, in her final scout around the library's perimeter, would collect them and promise him more.

"You just gobble them up, don't you?" she would say, beaming. "It's so inspiring to see someone your age who's so voracious for knowledge. I'll bring you a fresh batch tomorrow."

He was prepared to shuffle and reshuffle books from now to doomsday if that's what it took to be left alone, but then one afternoon toward the end of August, Miss Brint came to his table a bit earlier than usual, carrying a clipboard with a pad.

"May I put your name down, Mr. R.?" she said. She said it politely enough, but she didn't wait for his answer before scribbling something across the pad. "I was talking to Gloria this A.M., and you're the first person I thought of. 'Why, you should see how he pores through those books,' I told her. 'He's exactly the kind of example we need. He's a member of a minority grouping, and he's pulled himself up by his own bootstraps, and what could be a better example for these refugees?' You'll be an inspiration for them, Mr. R. We need a dozen literacy volunteers and you are our first."

Sex-starved, Rufus decided, not for the first time. He spent all night trying to put the word she had used before volunteer out of his head; it was as though one of the bugs he hated had followed him back to his room and was chirping beneath his bed. Next morning when Snipes frisked him, he did it more gently than usual.

"How are you this morning, teach? All set for class?"

In the station, his sense of trouble worked full-time. He could feel it, pick up the look of it, *smell* it, five or six tracks away. Two months of the library had been enough to take the edge off it, though. There were too many hidden corners—the books were piled too high, the carpet muffled too many sounds, and he was all the way to his table before he saw them.

Eskimos. Two of them. One, the man, sitting at the chair nearest the window. One, the woman, sitting at the chair nearest the stack. In between, one empty chair. His empty chair.

Rufus was too surprised to do anything but sit down. The woman smiled and made a little bow with her head; the man did the same. Neither one said anything. They sat with their hands folded on the table and stared straight ahead at the wall, imitating his posture. The woman was wearing a baggy gray dress with roses on the side; the man had on a green, short-sleeved shirt. They both smelled of almonds.

"Greetings," Miss Brint said, sweeping down the aisle with an armful of new books. She put one down in front of the woman, one down in front of the man, and one—a much bigger one—in front of Rufus. "May I introduce you formally? Mr. Rufus, this is

Kim-cha and Kim-choo, your new pupils. Kim-cha and Kim-choo,
this is Mr. Rufus, your literacy volunteer."

She accented their names on the second syllable, like someone
pretending to sneeze. Both of them bowed again—the man
mumbled something that sounded like "go fish." Rufus, for his
part, did what he always did when he felt threatened: he reached
toward the stack for a book.

Miss Brint laughed and took it gently from his hand. "You won't
have time for that today, Mr. R. The readers here will be hard
enough for them. Kim-cha and Kim-choo are new Americans. Our
goal is to provide them with the vocabulary that they will need for
life in their adopted land."

She leaned over his shoulder and opened the book to the last
page. There was a drawing of an American flag on top. Beneath it
were some words. "Of course, you don't get here until months
from now," she explained, "but I wanted to show you what we're
aiming for. It's their graduation piece. They're to go home and
write an essay on 'Why I Love America.' Won't that be insightful?
The committee's going to give a prize for the best one."

After Miss Brint had gone, Rufus examined the two of them
more carefully. They were twenty-five at most. The woman had a
body that was too plump for her face—it made him think of a
grape on top of a melon. The man, Kim-choo, was just the
opposite. His body was naillike and thin, his face moonlike and
full. They weren't Eskimos—he had seen pictures in one of the
books and they didn't have the same kind of bubbly smile. They
weren't Japs, and he didn't think they could be Chinamen—back
in the fifties, he had spent a week chipping grease from the bottom of a stove in a Chinese restaurant, and he knew a Chinaman
when he saw one. Their faces weren't yellow enough. Their skin
was olive color, so smooth that it looked like nylon. Their noses
and lips were on the small side and pushed together, and when

84   they looked at him, the edges curled and wrinkled in ways that he had never seen. He tried to think of what they reminded him of, and the moment he thought of it, he said it out loud.

"Monkeys."

Immediately, the man started smiling. "Munkays," he said, bobbing his head up and down. "Mun . . . kays."

The woman pursed her lips. "Mun . . . mun . . . kis," she said, frowning with effort.

"Munkays," Kim-choo said condescendingly. He leaned over so she could see his lips. "Munkays."

"Munkings?"

He shook his head. "Munkays."

"Munkays. Munkays, munkays, munkays."

Kim-choo mumbled something that sounded like "go fish" again, and they both smiled, as if they had just accomplished something fine. Rufus, though, smiled not at all. He stared silently out the window toward the police station, waiting for them to go away. He came to the library for quiet, and their eagerness disturbed it. Even when they didn't say anything, even when they just sat there wrinkling their lips and noses, he could feel it. Energy, enthusiasm, hope—they exuded it like a fizz. Cruising for a bruising, Rufus Junior would have said. Shark bait, lambs for the slaughter. "Fools," Rufus thought, but he didn't say anything this time, and when the clock reached twelve, the two of them got up and left.

The relief was only temporary. During the rest of the afternoon he felt the same ominous sensation that he had experienced the day barricades had gone up in front of the rest rooms at the station. He felt it when Snipes frisked him on his way outside, he felt it on the long walk back to his room, he felt it that night when he let out his landlady's cat, and he wasn't surprised to find the two of them there again in the morning, looking even more eager and excited than they had the day before. They had freshly sharpened pencils with them this time; beside the readers were crisp yellow pads. When Rufus sat down, they bowed at him, and this time he gave them the briefest of nods in return. He was nobody's fool. If the rules of the game had changed, they had changed, and if it took sitting there with them every day not to be thrown out, he would do it.

He opened the book.

The first page was covered with drawings of men, women, and children. The men were slightly taller than the women, the women slightly taller than the kids. They were dressed neatly in suits and ties, dresses and shorts. The men were getting into big cars outside big homes and waving goodbye. On the next page, one of the men was sitting at a big desk. Somehow, the woman had gotten to a store and was trying on a new mink coat. Underneath the pictures were words. Rufus stared at them for a second, shook his head in disgust, and pointed out the window to the police station.

"Slam," he said.

Kim-choo and Kim-cha were still concentrating on the drawings. He rapped his fist on the glass and pointed again.

"Slam."

"Slam," Kim-choo said, looking puzzled. "Spam," Kim-cha said, giggling.

A cop got out of a cruiser and stood there writing something against the hood. Rufus watched their eyes to make sure they noticed him.

"Fuzz," he said quietly.

"Fuzz," Kim-choo said. "Slam fuzz."

Rufus nodded. His approval set them smiling again—Kim-choo reached across the table and shook Kim-cha's hand. Their happiness irritated him. He waited several seconds, then pointed at the drawing of the businessman at his desk.

"Pig," he mumbled.

They had a harder time with this. Kim-cha couldn't pronounce the *P* sound. Rufus kept repeating it for them, jabbing his finger at the page.

"Mop," he said, turning to the next picture, the picture of a banker handing a farmer a loan. "Mop slops."

"Mop sops," Kim-choo said. He closed his eyes as if memorizing it, then stared at the picture and nodded. "Mop sops."

It was too fast for Kim-cha. "Spig," she said, turning back the page. "Spig."

"Mop slops and shit."

"Mop sops."

"Fuzz. Slam fuzz."

"Shit."

The pictures only got worse after that. There was a minister outside a church, a man pulling a lever on a voting machine, a judge sitting behind a bench.

"Lies," Rufus said.

He didn't wait to hear them repeat it. "Stay," he ordered, pushing back his chair. There was a stack of books near the men's room that he had leafed through earlier in the summer. Toward the far end of the bottom shelf was a faded paperback with red letters on the spine; he found it and brought it back with him to the table. The pictures were bunched together in the middle. The first was of Franklin Delano Roosevelt, the second was of someone he didn't know, and the third was of him, or at least someone close enough to have been him. Men waiting in line for soup in the thirties, caps pulled down over their eyes, collars turned up, blacks on the end. He grabbed the book by the edge and shoved it at Kim-cha's face.

"Me," he said. "Rufus."

They stared at the picture for a long time. Kim-cha scratched her nose.

"Me," Rufus said again. "Me, I."

"I?"

Rufus pointed to his heart. "I. I, I, I."

He showed them the tattered jackets the men were wearing, jabbed his finger at their shoes. But it was useless. As quick as they were to mimic him on the word, he could see the picture meant nothing to them. He opened the reader to the first page again and the letters printed across the bottom. It was the alphabet—he recognized the first three letters and the *R*—and by pointing to their pencils and then the page, he made them understand that they were to copy it.

They kept their heads cocked to one side over the table for the next hour, scribbling away. Kim-cha curled her tongue against the inside of her cheek and kept it there; whenever she came to a difficult letter, her cheek bulged out like a small ball. Kim-choo concentrated even harder, holding the pen with both hands, banging his fist against his forehead whenever he made a mistake. The following day, Rufus had them start all over again, and the day after that, they were already working when he sat down. Once they came to the end of the line, they would hand their pads to him for approval. Rufus would hold the paper sideways and turn it upside down, but the result was always the same: he grabbed his pencil by the middle and crossed their letters out with a thick black line.

The alphabet used up most of their time. Occasionally, he would add another phrase to those they had already learned, but only in response to one of their questions. In the middle of the reader was a picture of a man in dungarees shaking hands with a man in a suit and tie. Kim-choo pointed to it, and said something that sounded like "shinbone."

Rufus pointed to the picture. "This man here? Here?"

Kim-choo nodded. Rufus cleared his throat.

"Yes sir, boss," he said. "Yes sir, boss."

He made them repeat it until they said it right. As usual, Kim-choo got it first. He was quicker than she was, but more impatient, and Kim-cha would remember the words longer and pronounce them with more precision. Rufus noticed other differences during September. There was always something like rebellion in the way Kim-choo pointed to the pictures and demanded their sounds— there was something defiant and daring in the way he looked when Rufus crossed out their alphabets, too. Kim-cha, on the other hand, seemed determined only to please. Whenever Kim-choo became angry, she would put her finger to her lips, smile the sweetest of smiles, and say "shit" or "piss" or one of the other words Rufus had taught them.

The fall went on.

On Columbus Day, Kim-cha brought Rufus a rose; he pushed it gruffly to the side of the table, but that afternoon when he left, he took it with him. They wore the same clothes, even when it turned cold. Their lips became cracked—the salve they used made them look like minstrels. He would have them work on the alphabet until ten, then have them turn to the numbers. Before Thanksgiving, Kim-choo was sick; Kim-cha came alone and sat there staring out the window, twisting her hair. One afternoon Rufus followed them outside and walked behind them until they disappeared into a bus. Where did they live? Who was paying for it? It snowed in November. Miss Brint would glide down the aisles hugging herself tight enough to drive her thumbtack breasts in even further, but whenever she approached any closer, Kim-choo's almond smell would make her wrinkle her nose up and veer away, content to bestow upon them her most approving smile. Kim-cha had trouble with her L's. One morning Kim-choo came in and proudly spread a dozen new ten-dollar bills across the table; Rufus put eight of them in his pocket and handed back four. It snowed again on December first. Kim-cha had a trick of hiding chocolate bars beneath her dress; Rufus could hear the wrappers rustle whenever she scratched. In the course of the autumn he taught them these words: *porter, unemployment, dishwater, heartbreak, welfare, pain, underdog, hurt, whitey, scrub, scour, shoeshine, sick, tired, nightmare, no.* They were late one morning. Nine o'clock, ten o'clock. . . . When they finally arrived, he yelled at them without knowing why.

They were late again on the Monday before Christmas. Rufus had gotten to the library earlier than he usually did, and when he came around the stack to the table, they weren't there.

"Monkeys," he said bitterly.

He was mad at his own disappointment. To mask it, he reached into the stack for the nearest book, but it didn't have any pictures, and he had gone back to staring out the window when he heard a shuffling sound at the far end of the aisle.

It was Kim-choo, or at least his face; he was peeking around the next-to-last shelf. He waited until he had Rufus's attention, then came the rest of the way around with his surprise: a brand-new coat—an expensive red parka like skiers wore, with two zippers and a fur-lined hood. He had the hood puckered tight around his face; he pirouetted down the aisle like a model, smoothing down the nylon with his hands. Kim-cha was shyer. It was another minute before she found the courage to follow him, but when she did, she was wearing an identical coat to Kim-choo's, and smiling in the same smug, superior way.

"Where did you get those?" Rufus demanded.

They pulled the zippers up and down.

"Whitey been giving you those?"

They sat down without taking them off. Kim-choo's smile was even more insufferable than the one he had given him when he waltzed down the aisle. There was smugness in it, but triumph as well—triumph and liberation and revenge.

Very slowly, watching Rufus out of one eye, he leaned across the table and kissed Kim-cha on the cheek. "Love," he said, without a trace of accent. "L . . . O . . . V . . . E. Love."

"Where did you get that from? Who's been teaching you? I'm your teacher, you don't go getting words from nobody else, you hear me? You want words, you come see me. I want, I can flunk the both of yous. I can flunk you so bad they're going to kick you right back smack where you came from. Love? Don't go loving on me, man. I don't want none of that love shit around here. I don't want to hear about no love."

He could feel his heart pumping. He shoved the page with the alphabet at Kim-choo. "Here, copy those and do it quick."

Kim-choo stared down at the book and shook his head. "Why?" he said. "Why, why, why."

As infuriating as their coats were, as angry as he had become when Kim-choo had trotted out his new word, it was nothing compared to the rage he felt now. It wasn't as if Kim-choo was asking why they had to do the alphabet again. It was a bigger *why*, a *why* that took in everything. Why his coat was so threadbare and thin when they had obtained new coats so easily; why he let a bastard like Snipes go through his bag every morning; why he didn't tell Miss Brint to her face how dried-up and sterile she really was. But it wasn't just these *whys* either, it was *why* for his entire life. Why he had nothing to go back to but a narrow room with a dirty sink and a landlady that bullied him; why teenagers who ten years ago wouldn't have dared look him in the eye pushed him on the bus and laughed when he got mad; why, in the winter of 1933 in Boston, he had had to wait in line for a bowl of cold soup and give up his place whenever a white man arrived; why ever since he could remember he had worked and slaved for nothing; why his entire life had been one long lesson in shoving his bitterness back down his throat.

"Why, you want to know why!" he screamed. "Wait there, boy!"

He pushed his chair back and stumbled wildly down the aisle. A stack of cookbooks, a stack of kids' books, a stack of shit he couldn't be bothered with, then the one he wanted. Books on the bottom shelf where no one could see them. Books no one wanted. Pictures of the Depression, pictures of World War II, pictures of Korea, pictures of lynchings—he tore each book out from the shelf and threw it backward until he got to the one with the picture he wanted, the new green one, the one he went for when his anger was at its worst. Holding it like a football, he rushed back to the table and spiked it down before a startled Kim-choo.

"You want to see love? You want to see love, you start seeing. This is love. Love, you're going to see love. Love, love, love, love, love."

He slurred the sound into one long, wavering word. The pages stuck together. He ripped them out in handfuls, throwing them over his shoulder just like he had the books, not caring what the black bugs said, stopping only when he came to the picture.

"You want to see love, there it is. There it is. Look at it. Look at it, boy! Look at it good because I'm telling you that's love."

It was the only picture in color. On the right, shining like a tiny sun, a bottle of plasma. Looping down from it, a pink tube. Attached to the tube, a black arm. Above the arm, the soldier's face—bandages hiding the eyes, the lips curled back from the teeth, the mouth open and peculiarly round. The rest of the picture was in hazier focus as background. A black soldier in camouflage pointing to the sky, a fringe of jungle, mud the color of vomit, then the bottle again, the tube, the arm.

"Rufus Junior. Say it, boy! Rufus Junior! Rufus Junior! Rufus Junior! Rufus Junior!"

The force of it knocked Kim-choo back from the table. He was making furious bowing motions with his head, holding his hands in front of his chest in a desperate attempt to appease him.

"Wufus," he said frantically. "Wufus, Wufus, Wufus."

It wasn't enough. Rufus wanted to grab the book and throw it at him, but before he could, he heard another sound that was even louder than Kim-choo's stutter. It was a moaning sound. Not a moaning, but a crying. A crying and a moaning and a hum. A high-pitched, throbbing hum, the kind somebody made just before they had a fit, only this one didn't go away like fit sounds did, it became higher and more shrill.

Kim-cha was hugging the opened book to her breasts, rocking back and forth as though it were a baby she was holding, tears streaming down her face, her hair disheveled and wet. Rufus was so surprised that he left off screaming his son's name; Kim-choo, equally surprised, stopped trying to pronounce it, and the two of them sat there without moving, watching her grieve. She was oblivious to them. For all the attention she paid them, she could have been in the jungle herself, cradling the dead man's head. The sobs had total possession of her. She stared down at the picture, then hugged it again and began to wail, her body bending forward in the timeless, feminine posture of loss.

Kim-choo was the first to react. He went over to her, and put his arm around her shoulder and lifted her gently from the chair. She was crying even more now, but he managed to wedge her around the table to the aisle. They staggered past the reference section and the angry looks of the people reading at the desks. Long after they left, the sound of her sobs echoed through the bookstacks, and Rufus, in bending down to pick up the torn pages, found a patch of paperlike fabric that had fallen off her coat.

They didn't come the following day. They didn't come the day after that, either, and then it was Christmas and the library was closed. By the time New Year's was over, Rufus had gotten back to his old routine—the books taken at random from the shelves, the turning listlessly through the pages, the piling them at the end of the table, the staring out the window, and the naps. As it turned out, they did come back one more time. It was at the beginning of February, long after he decided he would never see them again. When he rounded the stack, he saw them sitting on either side of his chair just as they always did, their readers open in front of them.

They had changed since he last saw them. The chalky pink rash on their lips had spread over their faces; Kim-cha had cut off her long hair. Kim-choo didn't sit erect on the edge of the chair, but slumped wearily to one side, the way Manassa did whenever Snipes was about to hit him. Their coats had long tears in the side, and the fur on the hoods hung in strips. Neither of them looked at him when he sat down. They acted embarrassed and ashamed.

Rufus reached for Kim-cha's reader. He turned past the drawings of the huge automobiles and the generous bankers, the immaculate families and neat suburban homes until he came to the last page and the drawing of the American flag. He pointed to it, then to their pads.

"You write," he said, very slowly so they would understand. "You write."

Kim-choo nodded. The two of them reached for their pencils.

"Why," Rufus said.

"Why," Kim-choo nodded.

"I."

"I."

"Love."

"Love."

"America."

"A . . . Amarac . . ." Kim-choo stumbled over the word. He repeated it until he had the pronunciation right, but even then he said it with a question mark at the end, and he kept pointing at the flag and shrugging his shoulders.

"America," Rufus said, and he pointed out the window to the police cars and the ruined station. "America."

Slowly, sadly, Kim-choo began to nod. "America," he whispered. "Why . . . I . . . Love . . . America."

He put his pencil down. Kim-cha had the meaning of it now,

94 and she put her pencil down, too. They got up from their chairs and struggled into their coats. Their readers lay open on the table, but they made no move to pick them up. Without saying any-thing, without meeting his eyes, they walked down the aisle past the forgotten encyclopedias, turning left through the reference section just as they had the morning Kim-cha had cried, not arm-in-arm this time but apart, their shoulders slumped with the lessons they had learned, his prize pupils after all.

Narrative of the Whale Truck Essex

THE whale died somewhere in Kansas and it's a miracle we even got that far. The owners lost interest when attendance fell off and they began cutting back on the krill. The last shipment in Topeka had been a clear as weak consomme—its tail barely quivered when we pumped it into the tank.

I looked around for the telegraph office while Peter and the Whale Girl watched the convertible.

WHALE IS DEAD, I wired, WHAT HAPPENS NEXT.

Squires had kidnapped it the night before. When we got up in the morning the truck was gone. Two treads of yellow dirt leading off down the highway, a black stain where the tank had over-spilled. I'd been awake all night going over the latest charts. . . . It was complicated, I'd been putting it off. . . . It was 6:00 A.M. before I determined the whale wasn't breathing after all. That's when I ran out to tell Squires and that's when we found out about the kidnapping.

We had a milkshake in the drugstore. The man behind the counter said it was 1,242 miles to the sea. He had taken his kids there when they were small. After about an hour, I went back to the telegraph office. They'd already replied.

WHERE IS WHALE NOW.

The bastards, I thought. Just for that I'm not going to tell them.

We were in Alberta when the whale first got sick. There was a

96   sleevelike opening in the tank near one end. For a quarter you could stick your arm through a plastic valve and touch his skin. It was smooth—I never felt skin that smooth. A lot of them would make a face and quickly draw their arms away but Squires claimed he enjoyed being stroked.

We were in Banff for Indian Days. A rash broke out on just that one spot. White and pink rings that started to spread. We made them wear dish gloves after that. I got a prescription from a local vet but it only made it worse.

Squires was the technician. The girl wore net stockings. Pete handled the food—we all took turns driving the truck. What I basically had to do was monitor its heartbeat, digestive functions, respiration. Every once in a while stir the krill. Depending on my charts Squires would adjust the thermostat and oxygen flow to the appropriate level.

The tank was forty-three feet long. There were springs on the end so he could nudge the glass without its breaking. He'd do this a lot, especially around feeding time. By making a quarter roll to his right away from the viewing platform he could get some space to move his tail. But it wasn't much and by the time we got across the mountains he had given up moving at all. His brow would rise and fall slightly when he exhaled but that was it.

His spout was above the water, we kept it wet with a spray from a nozzle mounted on the roof. When it was cold his breath would freeze it shut and Pete would have to climb up there with a torch. A revolving green and blue strobe was mounted outside the glass near either eye. These, coupled with the bubbles of oxygen being pumped over his forehead, may have given him the illusion he was at sea. Sometimes his eyes seemed screwed up in pleasure like a cat's. When we camped near a stream that looked clean we would change some of the water, mixing it with bags of salt we kept locked in the pickup.

There were signs mounted along the walkway near each part of his body. Signs like you see in zoos, with spotlights aimed at the appropriate subject. "Flipper," one would say, going on to explain at great length the functions of the flipper. You would walk from sign to sign past unlighted intervals of blank, rippled skin and it made it seem like we had five or six animals in there, not just one continuous one.

The refrigeration system had broken down in Montana. We came close to losing him right there. I found some dry ice, Squires did something with the wires. But it must have been a turning point of some kind. Squires started to brood.

We moved the convertible so it was parked in the shade. The man ran out from the telegraph office waving a piece of paper.

WHERE IS WHALE NOW.

I handed it to the Whale Girl, she handed it to Pete, Pete tore it up.

The first two months we packed them in. Those days the girl still wore a dress—no one thought of calling her the Whale Girl until we got clear of the coast. People would line up for hours. High school bands marched us to town, mayors would pose near its tail.

If I had nothing better to do I'd help with the tickets. Even in those early days you could see the faces turning bored. We'd always had some demand their money back, but now people came out and began pushing through the waiting lines, warning everyone to go home.

The girl started her lecture when there were about twenty of them grouped near the door. There were earphones they could plug into either of two jacks set in the glass. Sometimes near dusk you could hear a remote squeaking. We didn't charge them for

98 this because a lot of time you couldn't hear anything at all. Squires would spend the night there, listening by himself.

THE WHALE IS THE LARGEST CREATURE THE WORLD HAS EVER KNOWN, she would say, AN IMMENSITY NEVER EQUALED. FABLED IN STORY AND LEGEND . . . pointing now to the Jonah and Pinnochio posters we had for sale on the wall . . . THE WHALE WAS ONCE SOUGHT FOR ITS OIL, CHASED ROUND THE WORLD BY MEN IN SMALL BOATS. GREATLY REDUCED, THE WHALE TODAY BATTLES GALLANTLY AGAINST EXTINCTION. IT IS ESTIMATED THAT RUSSIA AND JAPAN CURRENTLY ACCOUNT FOR OVER EIGHTY-FIVE PERCENT OF THE ANNUAL KILL . . . giggles, knowing frowns . . . THIS PARTICULAR WHALE CAME ASHORE IN OREGON THIS PAST SPRING, NO DOUBT DRIVEN THERE BY HIS PURSUIT OF THE GREAT SHOALS OF SHRIMP FOUND IN THOSE WATERS . . . guessing, not saying anything about the oyster-sized parasites they found in his ears . . . IT IS ESTIMATED . . . her voice rising a pitch . . . THAT THIS IS THE FIRST LIVING MEMBER OF HIS SPECIES TO BE SEEN IN THIS STATE SINCE OCEAN WATERS COVERED THE SPOT WE NOW STAND. IT IS FED ON PLANKTONLIKE CREATURES PUMPED IN THROUGH THE HOSE ON YOUR RIGHT . . . kids starting to fool around with the hose . . . LATER, SHOULD YOU CHOOSE, YOU MAY TOUCH THE ANIMAL'S SKIN BY PAYING THE APPROPRIATE AMOUNT NEAR THE INDICATED OPENING.

But by the time we got to Kansas her voice was bruised—she no longer bothered to recite it all.

WHALE, she would yell, TWENTY TONS. ALIVE! QUARTER A TOUCH . . . and people would still leave her to play with the hose.

One word of loss, one brief hint of regret and I might have gone after them. We were eating lunch in a cafeteria near the park when the telegraph man came by with another message.

WHERE IS WHALE NOW.

Pete dunked it in the gravy.

At every big town a shipment of food would be waiting for us in the railyard. I'd go to the bank and deposit the week's receipts. There would be a message telling us where the next shipment was going to be made and that's where we'd go. Other than that there wasn't any logic to it. We tried to hit all the colleges but it was summer and no one was around. The county fairs wanted too much to set up anywhere. We used to have to park out of town and run people back and forth in the pickup.

At one town we found a huge crate. Inside were three hundred immature gold fish wrapped in plastic bags. There was a note from the owners telling us to sell them as baby whales, three dollars each. We went into the bus station and flushed them down the john, fifty a flush.

The girl was polishing her fingernails. Pete mopped his head with a handkerchief. There were fans on the ceiling but they didn't work. The man sitting next to us tried halfheartedly to sell me a tractor—he acted relieved when I told him no. Somehow . . . in that heat, in that shadeless little town miles from anywhere . . . I had an intuition about Squires.

"He's taking him to the sea," I said. "He doesn't know he's dead and he's taking him home to the sea."

The girl got up to get some rice pudding. Pete just shrugged. I think he was waiting for me to suggest we chase after them. He said something about leaving the car behind, taking the pickup. A sixty-foot rig shouldn't be hard to spot. If the whale was still alive it might have been worth a try. I wondered how long Squires would listen for the squeaks.

No one actually saw the whale come ashore. Some kid found him on the beach at low tide. The coast guard tried to tow him back out to sea but each time they let go of him he started right back. By now the police were out to control the crowds. An ocean institute rushed up from L.A. for some tests—the truck was only to get him back to the center for some more. I'm not sure how the owners got their hands on him. Pete said it was in trade for a Seattle pier.

None of us even knew what kind of whale it was. We called him a sperm and left it at that. When attendance started falling off we were told to make him a killer. In each town we held a contest to give him a name, but we never found one we liked. Pete once stole a book of whales from the library, but the pictures weren't very good. The rash was pretty bad by then anyway.

I can still remember the Whale Girl's voice as she led them into the truck.

"It's a black whale," she said wearily. "It's a black whale and he never hurt anyone."

A man once drove up in a Caddy and offered to buy him. "Name your price," he said. . . . We used ammonia to clean the glass, a special salve on the hose. . . . Pete used to drive into town ahead of us and tack up the signs. . . . We got lost once near Cheyenne. . . . The posters bombed but we did well with the scrimshaw. . . . The Whale Girl sewed her own costumes. . . . When it was hot we used to leave the tent folded up and sleep next to the tank. The roar from the air pump reminded us of surf. . . . It snowed crossing the mountains. . . . We once drew eight thousand people in one day. . . . We never had any trouble with the government but the ASPCA once boarded us in Boise. . . . Squires would taste the krill before we pumped it in. . . . A cutthroat trout got into the tank when we were siphoning water out of the Yellowstone; it turned belly-up and died. . . . Pete once bet me fifty bucks I wouldn't get in the tank. I had stripped as far as my shorts before Squires found us. . . . If we parked facing the sunset it would turn the water red. . . . His heartbeat slowed in inverse ratio to our distance from the Pacific. . . . One day nobody came. . . . We woke up one morning to find a crack in the glass near its tail. . . . Squires once took a swing at me and broke his hand. . . . Whoever was driving the truck had to be careful about stopping short. . . . People used to knock on the glass to try and get his attention. . . . We pulled off at weigh stations to see how many pounds he had lost. . . . It bothered me to be alone with him. . . . Once we grilled steaks over a campfire—Squires actually sang. . . . We were on the road for 127 days. We traveled over ten thousand miles. We took good care of him but people were more interested in the truck.

We stayed in town all day. Before the banks closed I paid them both off. Pete took the pickup and the last I saw of him he was driving north. I told the Whale Girl she could have the convertible.

"What about you?" she said. It was the first time she had ever spoken to me. She still had on her stockings. I remember the breeze had come up and she was trying to keep her hair out of her eyes.

"Okay," I said and I got in beside her. I found out her name was Elizabeth and that she was a sophomore at USC. Unburdened, we drove all night across the plains.

For a while I expected to read in the newspapers about someone finding him. I still have the feeling I'm going to read about us all in a book someday. I even had that feeling before we left Kansas— the feeling that all I had to do was go up to anyone in the street, whisper "The Whale is dead," just loud enough so they could hear me, then sit back while the story spread. A casual mention those first weeks, picking up flourishes as it went from town to town, taking on different shapes to fit the mood of whoever held it for that day, spreading across the continent a month or two behind Squires, finally passing him, finally finding its way to someone

102   with the imagination to add some significance I could never quite
        capture myself, passed on by him to someone else with the
        patience it needs, passed from him just a step or two more. . . .
        Until years went by and this whisper emerged in a great book that
        had taken on everything—the prairies, the mountains, the sea at
        one end and maybe at two, Squires and the anonymous whale.
        An epic now, and I hadn't even whispered him a name.

Volpi's Farewell

THE sixth grade is doing *La Bohème* in English—an abridged version especially for children. Volpi sits in the principal's office waiting for the performance to begin.

"You have to be so careful in casting the students," the principal says, glancing down at a sheaf of test scores a secretary has just placed on his desk. "Your son is a good example of what I mean."

Volpi nods though he's hardly listening. The principal's window overlooks the playground which is empty this time of morning. A few limp jackets sway from the parallel bars, a half-inflated ball rolls back and forth in the wind.

"Ricky is much more sensitive than other boys his age. Perhaps Miss Heath was wrong in having him . . ."

"Miss Heath?" Volpi interrupts.

"Our music teacher. The one who was awarded the grant for her children's opera program. Perhaps she was wrong in having Ricky involved in something with a girl he's so obviously fond of. Sixth-graders take these things so seriously. It's hard for them to just pretend."

The principal always uses this tone of voice with the parents. But Volpi is flattered—he welcomes anything that makes him feel appropriately paternal.

"Mrs. Norion's class did a play about the presidents last year. She made the mistake of casting Tommy Hent as Abe Lincoln and when it came time for the assasination he punched John Wilkes Booth in the jaw. We had to stop the performance."

Volpi continues to stare out the window. A woman has appeared from somewhere to the right—his fiancée, a girl half his age. She takes off her coat, goes over to the seesaw and sits down on one end. She is wearing her hair in a ponytail—she starts fussing with it until it comes undone. From that distance she looks like a sixth-grader herself and Volpi can't help wincing when she takes out a cigarette.

"The boy will sing," he says, turning back to the desk to let the principal see he hasn't changed his mind. "I brought her especially down just to hear him. It's not as if Marcello loves the girl. It's Rodolfo who will love her. Ricky must realize this. He must realize tonight while he is still young."

Now it's the principal's turn to nod. He's rather taken aback by Volpi's voice—he's only heard it on records and had expected it to be much lower than it is. Volpi's son is playing Marcello and he has a crush on the girl who's playing Mimi. So far the rehearsals have gone badly. Volpi has graciously volunteered to oversee the last one that afternoon.

"Ricky gets along with the others but he broods," the principal says, scanning the one paper he hasn't let Volpi look at. "Perhaps . . . perhaps if he had a more settled environment at home."

"I no longer sing," Volpi says, with a slight wave of his hand. He says it automatically now—it has become his explanation for everything.

"Perhaps having a mother again. Someone much closer to Ricky's own age."

Volpi agrees that the principal is right. That is exactly why they had come down. Of course it would not be easy for a spirited young woman like her to have a stepson . . . they had quarreled once or twice about Ricky already, but . . . well, he could judge for himself. She was out there now if the principal would care to see.

But when they get to the window the playground is empty. No jackets, no ball, no fiancée. Volpi is forced to say something inconsequential about the grass.

"I heard you sing with Toscanini in 1952," the principal says just before he leaves. He says it in a rush, as if during all the time they were talking he had been trying to get up the nerve. "On the radio, of course. I'll never forget it. Your voice was so deep it rocked the china on my mother's end table."

Volpi acts puzzled. He rubs his hand across the glass, then clears his throat.

"No. It could not have been fifty-two. In fifty-two I was singing at Scala. Surely it was fifty-three?"

The principal shuffles through the papers. "Uh. . . . Yes. Yes, we're very honored to have you here, Mr. Volpi. On behalf of the students and faculty I would like to welcome you to Stewart School."

The two men shake hands formally and agree to meet in the auditorium at three o'clock for the dress rehearsal. Volpi walks down the corridor wondering if any of the rooms is Ricky's. He tries one of the doors—the children start giggling and he backs away without their seeing him. Further down the hall a girl tries to sell him a ticket. He buys two and doesn't take his change. When he finally gets outside to the parking lot his car is gone—there is no sign of his fiancée. He hurries over to the playground but no one is there either. For one crazy moment he considers following her footprints across the sand.

While he is trying to decide what to do the school lets out for lunch. Most of the children board yellow school buses. Two of the older boys start throwing someone's cap back and forth. They run closer and Volpi realizes it's a girl they are teasing. From the way she laughs, from the way she tosses back her hair, he guesses her to be that evening's Mimi.

Ricky is supposed to be meeting them at one o'clock but it is already half-past and no one is there. Two teachers stand guard by the bike shed, hugging themselves in the breeze. Volpi is about to ask them if they know where he could find Mrs. Palmer's class but a bell rings and they go inside.

The rehearsal is still two hours away but Volpi can feel the tension build in his throat, even though it will be his son who sings and not himself. Ricky has a good voice—there are possibilities in it already. But he is much too dreamy for a boy his age, as if he had inherited his personality not from Volpi but from one of the various romantic characters Volpi had once played . . . as if what was make-believe in Volpi had become real in Volpi's son.

Later, outside the auditorium, he finds a phone that works. He calls his fiancée's apartment. No one answers. He decides to wait twenty minutes before trying again but ends up calling every ten. Children go in and out the doors. The ones with solemn, self-important expressions are in the cast. A matronly looking woman walks by with sheets of music tucked under either arm. Miss Heath, he decides. She had been the one to write to him when the problem first developed.

He tries the phone again, then goes back out to the parking lot. There are a few stubby crocuses wedged in a grassy strip near the curb. As he stands there waiting he deliberately crushes them with his heel. *Ci lascierem alla stagion dei fior,* he whispers sarcastically. We'll part when the flowers bloom.

The rehearsal is half over by the time he gets there. The boys from the shop class are finishing up details on the gates of Paris. Miss Heath climbs a ladder and drops a handful of artificial snow. Off to one side in a pool of gold from the spotlight stands the girl he had seen in the playground. She is very much the prima donna. Her red hair is long enough to reach her waist and she is wearing a shawl. A group of gendarmes stands on the edge of her circle but the only one who dares come any closer is the Rodolfo. As the other children stare she takes him by the arm and whispers something in his ear.

Ricky is standing miserably off to one corner, trying hard not to look at her. He has his beard on and for some reason they have given him a stomach. It makes him look more the overfed bourgeois than the starving bohemian artist. He's much taller than the other boys but it only makes him awkward, something of a bully. His frustration makes him break his pencils in half during tests, leave class for no reason. As Volpi watches, Miss Heath goes over and says something to him. When he doesn't move she throws her hands up in disgust and goes back to coaching the chorus.

"Oh, there you are, Mr. Volpi. How are they doing? Not the Metropolitan, I take it."

It's the principal—Volpi has no choice but to follow him to the stage. He makes a great show of introducing him to Miss Heath and the children. Ricky cringes when the principal pronounces his name.

"Mr. Volpi has kindly offered to give us all some pointers. Perhaps you can show him your translation, Miss Heath."

There is a lull while they change scenery for Act Four. Miss Heath—whose voice seems to quiver between her teeth before sliding out—tells the principal that one of the soldiers is in love with the flower girl and that they have had to restage the Cafe Momus scene accordingly. Volpi takes the opportunity to ask how Ricky is coming along. She tells him everything appears to be under control now that he had gotten over the humiliation of having Mimi refuse the rose he had brought her. During the first rehearsal—as Mr. Volpi was undoubtedly aware—he had kicked Rodolfo in the stomach when it came time for the young lovers to kiss.

"But perhaps your being here . . ."

"I no longer sing," Volpi says, with that same little twist of his hand.

Miss Heath is not sure what he means but she nods and loans him her baton.

"Of course. Of course, Mr. Volpi."

They go through the fourth act for him. At first he stands half-facing the seats, expecting his fiancée to momentarily appear up the aisle. But despite himself the familiar music begins to capture his attention—he gradually turns until he's facing the set.

The Mimi is really quite good. She has a clear, steady tone and acts convincingly. The Rodolfo, on the other hand, is quite bad. He can't resist grinning at his friends in the chorus and has a habit of waving his arms over his head like a victorious prizefighter.

"Stop!"

Everyone looks around. It's the first time Volpi has interrupted.

"You are Rodolfo, no?"

The boy smirks—he starts to giggle.

"Is something funny? The girl you love is dying, is she not?"

Rodolfo grudgingly nods. He has seen the respectful way Mimi listens.

"Then stand over here. Like this. Sad. Remember. Very sad. And no laughing this time. Are we ready?"

They go back to the beginning of the death scene. Volpi positions them differently—the children look over to Miss Heath who nods in approval. He doesn't say much about their voices. If they feel it, he tells them, the voices will come. During all this time Ricky has been keeping as far away from Mimi as he can get without leaving the stage. Once he scowls at the fat little girl who plays Musetta and she runs off in tears.

"Marcello!"

Ricky looks up. Volpi waits until he has everyone's attention. He wants them to see he plays no favorites.

"This is the most important phrase in *Bohème*. Mimi is dead. Rodolfo—your best friend, Marcello—has just realized this. Soon everyone cries. You must give them some reason to live. *Coraggio!* Can you sing that for me please?"

Miss Heath clears her throat. She leans in front of Volpi and points apologetically toward the score.

"A thousand pardons, gracious lady! Courage! In English, of course. But you sing it just the same. Bravo. May we have some music please? Marcello?"

Ricky just stands there. He rolls his tongue against the side of his cheek.

"Sing please."

Ricky sticks his hands in his pockets. Mimi giggles from her deathbed and he turns a bright red.

"Sing!"

He mumbles something. Volpi has him do it over again. For twenty minutes they go over this one phrase while everyone stands around in embarrassment. Volpi is never satisfied—he tells him it must ring! It must ring in their hearts long after they go home! But this only makes Ricky stutter even more. When he starts walking off the stage Volpi grabs him and pushes him back. The boy whispers something no one but Volpi can hear. Asking you-know-what, they assume—now the rest of the girls start to giggle. But to everyone's amazement Volpi suddenly leans down and slaps him across the face.

"Idiot! She is no business of yours! You will never be a singer! Never!"

For a moment no one can move. Miss Heath rubs at a speck of dirt that has somehow gotten caught in the keyboard. The principal wipes his glasses off on his tie. Mimi looks toward Volpi as if it is her face he has slapped. Ricky stares at him too—on his face is a knowing smile, as if he had been expecting it all along. In the middle of the stage Volpi is shaking with anger. Motion resumes—he wheels around, breaks the baton in half, stalks majestically out of the auditorium as the uproar begins.

Five hours go by. Volpi is sitting by himself in an empty class-room. The desk is much too small for him and his knees bang against the top. For the last hour he has never taken his eyes off the ceiling. He already knows how many holes there are but now he counts them again. Earlier he had heard car doors slam as parents arrived for the performance. A janitor comes by with a flashlight and shines it under the door.

There are pictures hanging near the windows. One of them is of a valentine and a horse. Next to it is a poster showing the various constellations. Volpi goes over to the blackboard and starts to write something, then changes his mind and puts the chalk back down. He starts humming instead. He hums from *Rigoletto*, then *Manon*, then *Faust*. He can't bear the thought of going home to an empty house, he can't bear the thought of going back to the auditorium. He hums the baritone roll from *Butterfly*, he hums from *Bohème*—he can't bear thinking about the past and now, for the first time in months, he has no particular hope in the future. As he stands there he hears music coming from one end of the corridor. For a moment he thinks he's imagining it but then he hears it again. Music followed by applause.

Despite everything the performance is going well. Miss Heath plays the piano with feeling. The principal is backstage keeping the soldiers in line. The poet Rodolfo has already met Mimi the seamstress. They have sung of their love in the garret, they have sung of their love again in the cafe, they have sung of their love as the snow falls, vowing to stay together until spring. The other bohemians laugh and sing—the fat little girl who plays Musetta waltzes about like a born Parisian and when she sings how beautiful she is her face begins to shine.

But by now Mimi is coughing and when Act Three ends she falls in a faint across the stage. The audience becomes increasingly quiet. Whether it is the power of the story—the young innocence of the boy and girl who play the doomed lovers, the effect of the falling snow—they begin to feel themselves strangely moved, as if it were all quite real.

The curtain goes up for the final act. Marcello and Rodolfo dance around the stage only to be interrupted by Musetta who brings in the dying Mimi. Colline rushes out to sell his coat for medicine. The young voices join together—for a moment it seems that all will end in perfection.

But it soon becomes obvious that something is wrong. Ricky has been acting strange through the act. He pauses between words—he seems to be having trouble controlling his voice. When he is supposed to be sadly drawing the window curtains he goes over instead and kneels by Mimi's bed. Miss Heath whispers something from the piano and he staggers back in place.

Suddenly the music stops. The muff falls from Mimi's hands. The bohemians realize she is dead and now—turning around in disbelief—Rodolfo realizes she is dead as well. He rushes over to the bed. The music swells . . . the music swells . . . the music swells. . . .

Nothing happens. Marcello has missed his cue.

"Ricky!" Miss Heath whispers.

But he doesn't hear her. It's been too much for him. Crying in anguish he runs over to Mimi's bed, too, pushing away the startled Rodolfo and falling in tears across the motionless body of his beloved.

"Coraggio!"

Volpi's voice booms out from the back of the auditorium like a benediction—over the parents, over the footlights, over the music which, the phrase finally sung, swells to completion as the curtain falls. No one applauds. They are too moved for applause and in that strange hush the voice rings without diminishing, as if by its

112   compassion and force it can somehow outlast all the heartbreak, all the pain and disappointment that will be theirs in the years to come.

The voice finally fades. The lights go on. The parents very quietly go up to the stage and take their children by the hand.

North of Peace

ARE there laundromats in Russia? Little machines that vend coarse Soviet soapsuds, changemakers for reducing rubles into kopecks, huge Socialist dryers? Sanders wondered about this every time he pulled the peace van into a new Wash N' Roll or Suds Bucket or Mr. Kleen. He'd like a crack at one if there were. He could picture the thick Olgas and stolid Ilenas leaving their tubs and coming over to him in twos and threes—shyly at first, in awe of the white dove painted on the van's side, poking each other in hearty Russian ways, finally speaking to him, reaching over for a leaflet, the light, colorful one on a mutually verifiable freeze.

But he wasn't in Russia now, he was in Vermont, and his clothes hadn't been washed in over a week. There had been a rally in Brattleboro on Monday, weekend peace fairs in Burlington and Montpelier. He had intended to head back down to Boston for a refit after that, but a priestly looking man named Smith had stopped him outside the State House and begged him to come to a supper his church was having to raise money for a tax-resisters' fund. Sanders had driven north all morning to get there, coaxing as much as he could out of the clutch. When he came up over the last hill mentioned in the man's directions, he found not a church promised him, but a pig sty—a pig sty dominated by a crudely lettered sign, "AMERICA OUT OF U.N.!"

There wasn't much he could do about it. He let Spacehead out

114 for a run with the pigs, then cranked the ignition up and started
south. He was completely lost now. This was a part of Vermont
he had never seen before or read about. There were no colonial
homes or prim village commons, not even any road signs or res-
taurants. Occasionally, he would pass a lopsided cabin or trailer,
their sides bound together with bailing wire like crates that would
otherwise burst, but other than that, the landscape was empty.
Sick-looking trees, indecisive hills, abandoned farms—that was it.
West Virginia, only worse.

Skilton was the name of the town that finally appeared. It was
one of those places that mocks itself, the proud Corinthian town
hall testifying to the high hopes that were once entertained there;
the collapsed pillars and blistered paint testifying to the dream's
end. There were some old men on a bench beside the last intact
pillar, their shoulders hunched as if the weight of the ruins were
upon them. Up the street, younger men as pale and cold as their
stubby cigarettes turned to look at the van as it went past. One
man, quicker than the rest, shouted something and spat.

"Ah yes," Sanders said, slowing down. "Your basic good-old-
boy redneck, Vermont variety. See him, Space? A self-deluded
tool of the complex. Here I am trying to save his life and he spits."

If he was going to be mobbed, he might as well be mobbed in
style. He drove past the empty stores at a crawl, giving those few
who were around a good look at the dove, the "Give Peace a
Chance" sign, the California plates. He waved to both sides like
the Pope, goosed Spacehead until he barked, beeped rhythmically
on the horn.

"Skilton, Vermont. My kind of town!" he sang, but as suddenly
as he began, he stopped and yelled fiercely at Spacehead whose
bark had soared into a howl. It had happened before like that; one
moment he was full of energy and confidence; the next, he was
lonely and depressed.

He stopped at the laundromat more to wash out his mood than

his clothes. It was in one half of the old train station; rusted washers lay canted across the tracks outside, as if to barricade and trap any train that stumbled into town. He tied Spacehead to the steering wheel, then climbed in the back and threw everything white, crumpled, or otherwise soiled into the knapsack. With his missionary optimism, he took along some leaflets and thicker booklets: "The Medical Effects of Thermonuclear War:" "If a Bomb Fell on Omaha;" and "Nuclear Free Existence," this last written by himself.

A blast of hot air hit him as he went through the station door, carrying with it a smell of ammonia, dampness, and old gum. It was hard to believe that a place so dirty could be devoted to cleaning—the walls were covered with the kind of knobby purple scum that grows on boats; the floor was a garden of dust. He stopped by the first washer to get his bearings. The half-dozen or so women sitting on the waiting room benches glanced up at him with a look that was curious and spiteful at the same time, trigger-happy cowboys into whose saloon he had just strolled. He smiled to show he meant no harm, unshouldered the pack onto the folding table and went in search of the change machine.

There wasn't one. There wasn't a detergent machine either.

"I give up," he said, throwing his hands up with a little laugh.

None of the women smiled. They had gone back to watching their dryers, staring toward the foggy round windows with TV intentness. Sanders noticed they were all wearing heavy rubber boots, even though it was May; it made him feel they knew something he didn't.

"Carefully, Peter," he said to himself.

He quickly appraised the six women. The young blonde with the screaming boy looked like a possibility, but he couldn't make any move in that direction without being thought a seducer. He decided he was better off with the oldest, the one whose plastic curlers looked like solidified pink turds.

"Excuse me, ma'am?"

Her eyes remained on the clothes.

"I can never remember. Am I supposed to put my white stuff on hot or cold?"

Though she was sixty, she was chewing gum, or what he thought was gum; shifting it to the other side of her cheek, she spat a greenish juice toward the floor, then wiped her mouth off on her sleeve with a daintiness that was endearing. Sanders, as he often did when talking to someone smaller, knelt down beside her, as if by doing so he could make his huge bulk correspondingly inoffensive and meek.

"Hot, eh? That's what I figured. You put bleach in with light stuff?"

She ignored him. She put the back of her hand against the dryer window with the gesture of a mother testing her child's fever.

"No bleach. Okay. You'd think I'd know by now. I've been on the road, let's see. . . . Well, almost two years now. Lots of people figure I'm a traveling salesman when I tell them that, and in a crazy kind of way I am."

Behind them, the little boy had climbed one of the washers and was pounding on its lid with his shoe. Sanders glanced angrily over at him. He had a cut on his cheek that was yellow and ready to burst.

"I'm selling peace," Sanders said, his voice rising over the din. "I'm selling the idea it's about high time all the mothers and grandmothers in this world speak up for themselves and tell these generals that our kids are not going to be the innocent pawns in their thermonuclear delusions. As a matter of fact, I have some absolutely free literature here that explains in detail what . . ."

"Peace" had been enough to boost the woman to her feet, and at the word "thermonuclear," she fled, cradling against her bosom an armful of wet bras.

"Like I say," Sanders mumbled.

He looked over to see if she had scared anyone else away. Four of the women were already folded and stacked, but the younger one still had things in the wash. He scattered three of the leaflets on the table with some old *Field and Streams*, added several to the rack set up by the Jehovah's Witnesses, then went down the aisle to an empty machine and began stuffing in his clothes without bothering to separate the colors. There was enough quarters in his pocket for one good-sized load; a few seconds later, he was staring at the spinning fabric with the same concentration as the women.

Except for the kid's whines, it was peaceful in the laundromat. The repetitive drum of the machines had a narcotic effect, and it felt good to be working at something so basic and normal—so good and soothing and normal that it ended up frightening him. Times like this, he would lose track of his task, feel it slip away from him into the balmy, gentle light of his childhood, and he would have to force himself to remember the missiles and warheads and bombs. After this came a swing the other way; remembering, the horror came back in redoubled strength, and he sat bolt upright on the washer with the abruptness of a sentry who has just caught himself falling asleep.

He checked the other machines. Except for the blonde girl, everyone had left.

"Boy, there must be an easier way," he said, smiling.

The girl didn't look up. She was eighteen or nineteen—twenty at most. Put the kid at four, and she had married at fifteen. She still had enough of a figure to show why the boys had been after her, but there were hollow spaces beneath her eyes the color of bruises, and when she straightened up, her right shoulder was noticeably lower than her left. On the table next to her were six heavy baskets of unwashed clothes.

"The part I hate is waiting for everything to dry. You'd think they'd invent a microwave or something to do it faster."

The girl looked at him this time. She seemed puzzled, and Sanders realized that she didn't know what microwave meant.

"It's like a toaster thing," he said gently. "It uses radiation."

She took his explanation in with the expression of a child grimly
accepting a new toy. He was going to explain more, but she was
turning, yelling listlessly at one of the baskets.

"Get out of there, Howard. You hide one more time, momma's
going to slap you."

The boy exploded from the heap of clothes and galloped off
toward the nearest dryer. Sticking his head inside, he started
screaming, testing the echo.

"Cute kid," Sanders said.

She looked at him like he was a fool.

"Can I buy him a Coke or something?"

"Give him iodine is more like it."

"Uh, right."

Flustered, Sanders began his spiel too abruptly.

"You'd think I'd be used to washing my own clothes by now,
wouldn't you? I've been on the road, let's see. . . . Well, going on
two years now. I go around the country selling the idea it's about
high time all the young mothers in this country speak up and tell
these generals down there in the Pentagon that kids like that one
over there aren't going to be sacrificed to their thermonuclear
ambitions."

"Get out of there, Howard."

"I've got some booklets on it. This one explains what would
happen if a one-megaton bomb fell on a city twenty miles from
here." He hesitated. "Are there any cities twenty miles from
here?"

"St. Johnsbury," she said, frowning. "They can bomb it every
day in the week and twice on Sundays for all I care."

"Right. Well, this other one. . . . Hey, he's got quite a set of
lungs there, that last one was a classic!. . . . This other one details
some of the efforts women like you are making a Greenham Com-

mon in England and so on to end nuclear madness. It's more upbeat than the first one."

"How much?"

"Free. Here, take one."

"Nothing's free." She pushed another quarter into the dryer. "Get going machine," she said, hitting it.

Howard had his scream down pat now, and the empty drum of the dryer gave it enough bass that it seemed the deeper, terrified scream of a man. His mother yelled something at him as mechanically as before, then started tugging clothes from the nearest basket. She did it slowly, holding up each different article in front of her as if they were exhibits in some explanation she was trying mutely to get across. Sanders wasn't sure what it was. Still, he watched her with renewed interest. In the last three months he had spoken to group after group, and it seemed a novelty to have only one pair of eyes to focus on, one face to study. When she leaned over the washer, her shirt rode up over her waist—her skin was as pale and soft-looking as a baby's.

"What are you looking at?" she demanded. She brushed the hair back out of her eyes.

"I just wondered why you pushed everything down so tight."

She pointed toward his machine. "That's why, smartypants."

The unbalance light was on. Water was oozing out of the top and running onto the floor.

"Jesus! Don't do this to me!" Helpless, Sanders tried to scoop the water back in with his hands.

"Push it down."

"What down?"

The girl brushed past him, and stuck both arms into the machine up to her elbows, shaking the clothes apart with the severe, expert motion someone would use in throttling a pig. Miraculously, the light went off; the machine gurgled again in contentment.

"Thanks."

The girl didn't hide her satisfaction. "You sure don't know much about lawndraying."

"I'm basically a dirty old bum. Look, I'm sorry if I sounded stiff before. I speak in public a lot, but it's not the same thing."

"You a TV minister? Wasn't for that beard, you could."

"I work for the Freeze Now coordinating committee down in Boston. I drive my van around the country meeting with small groups of people who are concerned about nuclear war. I've got a sleeping bag, a radio that doesn't work, three rusty can openers and a dog named Spacehead."

She laughed, but instantly stopped. Sanders had never seen anyone choke off their joy so quickly and deliberately.

"But anyway, that's what my life is all about. I have this fear. . . . What's your name?"

"Mrs. Lisa Cooper."

"I have this fear, Lisa, that the world is going to blow itself up, and this fear goes with me wherever I go. The only way I've. . . . Boy, that screaming is getting to my head. Is there any way we could pipe him down a few octaves?"

"Howard!"

"But like I say. The only way I've ever found to deal with fear is to make directly for it, get right smack in the center of it and start hitting away. That's why I talk about it even with people I meet casually, like yourself. We need more fear. Either men and women like us change our hearts and say no to war once and for all, say no in the next few months, or it's all over, simple as that."

He started telling her about the cruise missile, and how its deployment would make a verifiable freeze impossible, about the Pershing II and the instability it would cause, about the SS-20, but even as he marshaled the familiar arguments, he knew it was useless, that the girl would continue to stare at him as blankly as she had when he mentioned the microwave. Without stopping, he began talking instead of the people he had met on his journey,

how concerned they all were—how a professor in Oregon had
confessed to him his fear for his infant daughters, how the man's
voice had trembled as he talked; how a doctor in Ohio had invited
him into her home and begged him for ways she and her family
could help put an end to the threat; how once in Michigan a
parade of young and old people alike had formed behind the van,
following him to a park where they sat in a circle and listened as
he talked—how much fear and anger and bewilderment he had
seen in their faces, and how much hope. He talked faster than he
usually did, losing the calm, matter-of-fact tone the committee
had drilled into him, wanting nothing more than to move this one
defensive and battered human heart. It was as if all his journeying
came down to this—the girl voluntarily taking a leaflet from his
hand.

At times he thought he was getting through to her, then
Howard would start peeing into the washer or sprinkling detergent on the laundromat's cat. He had pulled his pants down.
He skipped around with his brown, pointy bottom doing as much
damage as he could.

The girl didn't chase him anymore. She stood with her hands
on her hips near the biggest dryer, studying Sanders in an ex-
pressionless way that could hide anything.

"Finished?" she said.

"We all have to band together."

"I said are you finished?"

Sanders shrugged.

"Okay, so now you can listen to me." She yanked the dryer
door open, stuck in her arm. "Know what that is?"

"A pillowcase."

"It's a diaper. It's a diaper for my Janet who is right now six and
a half years old. Six and a half and she still needs a diaper, the
doctor can't tell me why."

She bent down again. "Know what that is? That's Howard's

over there cowboy shirt. His grandmom bought him that at the K-Mart down in Barre when he was two and it still fits. The boy don't grow, mister. He screams and hollers and it uses him up and he don't grow."

Howard, hearing his name, started banging the dryer doors.

"These are jeans. They are jeans for my husband, my brother, my Dad and God knows who else. I wash jeans, mister. That's all I do. I wash them on Tuesdays and Thursdays and Fridays, and sometimes on Sundays I get to wash underwear. I don't get to travel around in fancy vans. I've never been to Orygon or Ohio or places like that. I go to St. Jay once a month to pay the doctor for telling me Janet's abnormal, then I come home in time for my old man to wallop me. That's what I do. . . . Howard!"

The boy ran past her—she made a grab for him, but missed. He was up on the bench beside her, up on the chair, up on the washers. He spread his arms apart as far as they would go, sucked in a lungful of air.

"Kaboom!" he yelled. "Kaboom! Kaboom! *Kaboom!*"

He hurled the last one out, throwing his arms apart even further, putting such violence into it that it scared him, and he began wailing and choking and crying.

"Howard! I warned you."

"I know all that," Sanders said, talking over the boy's screams. "I know life is tough, but we have to forget about that for now, save the world first, *then* come back to setting it right. It's now or never, Lisa. It's *now*."

Whether it was the urgency in his voice, or something he had said, her eyes for the first time met his—met them directly, without any suspicion in between.

"You still have one of those booklets?"

"Sure."

"Give it to me."

Sanders felt a surge of joy. "I wrote this one," he said. He held it in front of him like a flower.   *123*

She took it—she wiggled it appraisingly back and forth, then shook her head.

"That bigger one. Quick."

He gave it to her. She rolled it tightly in her hands, and with a gesture oiled by long practice, reached up and hit Howard across the face.

Spitfire Autumn

THE funny thing is neither of us had even seen a Yank before much less danced with one. Here he was, a little dark man on crutches standing in the corner of the pub chewing a chocolate ice cream where what we expected was a tall dreamy cowboy with pistols and high boots. The very first Yank for two runaround girls of eighteen, and he turns out looking underfed, underpaid, and under-you-know-what, not the other way around like everyone was saying. But what was so extraordinary was he was *chewing* on the ice cream, not licking it like anyone else would have done.

"I'm going to dance with him," Angel said, just like that.

"You can't!" I said for no particular reason except my being there to watch out for her. That and because seeing all those brown uniforms for the first time sent shivers all down my spine and I couldn't think very clear.

What you have to remember was that to Angel and I, growing up south of the river, the West End was just as far-off and foreign as Texas or California or anywhere else. And I'd lost my mum in a raid you see. They'd taken her away to hospital during the night, and since Mrs. Williams next door was already gone off to work and I was the oldest they had me wait by the tube station for my dad coming home. They gave me a piece of paper with the name of the street on it in case I forgot. Dad changed after that. I don't think it was her dying so much as the time he had trying to get across the burning city to where she was. It took him the better part of all day, and when he got there it was too late.

But what I intended to say was that for a lot of girls like Angel and I coming on to be eighteen or so the West End in those years represented heaven and all we could think of was someday getting there. Here we were cooped up in the Depression, then the Blitz, all the young men gone off, our baby brothers and sisters out in the country, not knowing if we would even make it to seventeen much less eighteen, stuck there to rot in school with nearsighted masters who coughed and got the blackboard all moist so you couldn't properly write your sums without the chalk slipping. . . . Here we were and not ten minutes away by underground was paradise swarming with Yanks and money and bright lights and all the things we'd ever dreamed about.

It was too much for a lot of the girls—a lot of them went out on the street straight away. And it's a wonder Angel didn't, too, because she was that type of girl in some ways. Wild like, full of fun, always needing new clothes and lipstick her mum and dad couldn't possibly afford. They were terribly strict besides, and of course that's what made half of them do it in the first place.

I suppose we must have looked that kind, God knows, all fancied up in nylons we'd practically stolen for, out the first time for ourselves in Piccadilly, and here Angel is going up to ask a Yank who's at least four inches shorter than she is to dance.

"Wish to hell I could, babe," he said, a little Adolf mustache under his nose from the ice cream.

I'm not sure what Angel said after that. There were a lot of Tommys there, too, and one of them was giving me the business. Polite like but you knew what he wanted. In those days it was always "Let's you-know-what, Kay, we don't have much time." After the war it was always "Let's you-know-what, Kay, we have to make up for lost time." Nowadays, nowadays when all most of them should be thinking about is a nice warm chair in front of the fire and a quiet read it's the "Let's you-know-what, Kay, we don't have much time" all over again.

But anyway the next I knew they were really dancing, Angel and the Yank. He still had his crutches with him—he was leaning on her shoulder while she held him up, the two of them swaying back and forth to a slow dreamy Vera Lynn. But then a fast lindy came on, the kind Angel liked, and she ran over and handed me his crutches to hold and sure enough they started whirling around the pub like Fred Astaire and Ginger Rogers, Angel laughing and the Yank with a big surprised grin on his face matching her step for step.

I don't know what would have happened when the music stopped because just then the Yank's sergeant came back from the gent's. You can imagine how he must have felt, one second his friend standing there as forlorn as can be, the next waltzing across the room with a beautiful blonde. The sergeant started yelling and pointing trying to get everybody's attention so they could see what was happening. The barmaid had been watching all along, too, and now she started pulling all the dancers apart trying to make room for Angel and her Yank.

"Pardonmel'vegottorun," I said to poor Tommy just as fast as that. "Scuseme," I said. "Scuseme," pushing my way through the crowd. "Come on, Vee, let's go!" I whispered, grabbing her by the back of the sweater and tugging her toward the door. All along we were supposed to be visiting my sister Flora in Lambeth, and there's no telling what her parents would have done if they found out where we really were.

But anyway what I wanted to say. . . . That was Angel's first Yank, September 10, or maybe 11, 1944. The newspapers only caught up with her after the second one in October so all along their tally was wrong, one behind if you see what I mean. Actually it should have been seven miracles by V-E Day, not the six they finally credited her with.

We were all so excited and giggly it never occurred to us it *was* a miracle. All we could think was here she had actually danced with a Yank and not only a Yank but a Yank who chewed chocolate ice cream. It was too early to go home yet so we started down toward Trafalgar Square, arm in arm, like two little Alices lost in Wonderland. It was all the crowds, you see, all the different colored uniforms pushing by us smelling soft and warm in the rain. We felt anything could happen and at the same time felt safe and secure for the first we could remember, as if nothing could touch us here in the crowd, not the raid sirens we heard in the distance, not the bombs, not the thought of ever having to go back across the river.

The streets are just as crowded today, of course, but it's not the same at all. I remember those old posters warning us that if we didn't keep our lights off, if we didn't save tin and petrol, if we whispered to the wrong person. . . . If any of those things happened or didn't happen, the streets of London would be crowded with Germans and Japanese and Italians, and here it is thirty-two years later and they *are* crowded with Germans and Japanese and Arabs and God knows who else, even though no one I knew ever whispered or wasted a thing. A man on the telly said you could tell a native Englishman because he walked on the outside of the footpath away from the tourists. Well, out in the bloody street is more like it today, there being no room in near the shop windows for any except foreigners scurrying from store to store with their packages like they were looters sacking Oxford Street.

It's funny thinking how things change and how little, too. Here Angel was so beautiful and yet she never married, though there were dozens who would have had her and one or two nearly slit their throats they couldn't. I wasn't half that pretty and I tied the knot before the war was hardly over, Jack and I having forgotten to be careful one night when the buzz bombs were coming down. Angel was my bridesmaid of course and I remember everyone saying well, it won't be long before that one's a bride, you can bet a fiver on that. But she never was. And yet here I am today, Jack dead, Ronny and Carol both gone off to Australia, me just as alone as Angel ever was, as if all that family and marriage and pain and joy business never happened, had just been a dream.

Angel changed a lot after the war. She was never what you would call The Brain Trust sort, but she got so she was absent-minded and you had to tell her a thing twice or so before she really heard you. And then it almost seemed she was deliberately being mean to her old self some of the things she did. It was like she didn't want to remember any of those times anymore, wanted to deliberately spoil the memories so she wouldn't be tempted remembering.

The job she took when she was made redundant at the office, her boss being Pakistani and having a sister just over he put in her place, is a good example—a dance instructor part-time in a studio near Paddington. It could make you cry seeing her go off to work all fancied up looking not all that different from the way she looked in the war. I mean here was a woman men had actually *prayed* to dancing every afternoon with Jamaicans and Indians and whoever came in off the street wanting to learn the fox-trot or the waltz or whatever. She said she didn't mind—we made a joke of it, comparing her foreigners with mine, me working as a shop assistant at Marks and Spencer at the time. She liked West Indians best, she said. They would forget to be shy after a while, giving themselves completely over to whichever dance it was they were doing. The Arabs you had to be careful with because they weren't supposed to be there to begin with so you knew they weren't the good kind. She didn't like the way they kept staring at her legs.

Poor Angel. I felt so sorry for her the last few years only she would get mad and refuse to say anything if she caught me at it. She was never one to reminisce about the old days was Angel. The only thing was you couldn't say anything bad about Americans

130   and God help you if you did! That and the habit she had of looking off toward the sky saying "Well, Kay dear. Looks it's going to be a real Spitfire autumn this year," the same way that some people watch the leaves in Regent's Park and predict winter's coming. We'd walk arm in arm like when we were girls and for a time we'd both get good and misty-eyed. "Yes," I would say, "Yes, it's a real Spitfire autumn this year all right," feeling nostalgic and sad, though I was never sure what there was in the air made her say that.

She had a horror of souvenirs—after she died last October I was surprised finding out she'd kept any. There were the newspaper cuttings and some badges and insignia her Yanks tore off their tunics to give her while they were dancing. She left them to me, mainly because she was afraid her niece's husband Mickey would get them if she didn't. Angel lived with them her last few months because she couldn't afford anywhere else. Sally was all right, always the smile, always the kind word when I came to call. Mickey was something else again, always dressed in expensive suits, ingratiating like a baby lamb if you were someone better off than he was, lording it over Angel because she was stuck but giving her the eye from time to time, too, because she was a handsome woman still at fifty-one and you could see heads turning when she walked down the Bayswater Road on her way to work.

I'm not sure what Mickey's actual job was—something to do with antiques he claimed. But what he really did was go around buying up old war medals from RAF fliers or navy officers who had fallen upon hard times, selling them in turn to German collectors who were willing pay a pretty penny for them. Mickey made a bundle on it I suppose. And I suppose the fliers got something out of it, too, which God knows they deserve the stingy way the government treats them. But what I hated so was his manner, him sitting there bragging about the Victoria Cross he had all wrapped up in his coat pocket and how he was meeting this rich German solicitor in the Ritz that afternoon to complete the deal, except he never called it a deal he called it a "transfer." It got so after a while I had Angel meet me down below in the street. He was the kind of man who's old enough to remember but who won't, and I've always thought that's the worst sin of all for us.

But anyway what I meant to say before I got started was we never learned the name of that first Yank. We wouldn't have known the names of the others either if it hadn't been for the newspapers—Angel, for all her madcap ways, being too shy to actually come right out and ask them. The articles would have their hometowns and how long they had been in the service and what they were going to do when they got out which was always something silly like eat the biggest steak in Kansas City or sleep till noon every day of the week. Sometimes when there's nothing on the telly at night I take her scrapbook out and read them off trying to match the right name to the right face to the right club. . . . Read them right out loud like that and it brings it all back. . . . The soldiers calling out to us on the street, the girls who wanted to signaling back to them from off in the dark holding matches up to their faces. . . . The curly cigarette smoke that used to leak out the cracks near the window and let you smell the canteen before you were even across the street to it, the wall of music that hit you when you opened the door and maybe it was Tommy Dorsey they were playing and maybe it was someone else, but how it seemed another door you had to walk through before you belonged, seal-ing you in once you *were* through, in with uniforms packed so tight you wouldn't think there was room for one more, the two of us getting up on tiptoe to see while the lady took our coats, the middle of the room seeming to tilt back and forth which was the only way you could tell people were dancing, that and the glimpses we had of tops of men's arms looping over tops of girl's heads as they turned them out into the crowd and brought them

132   back again into their arms. . . . How the floor was always wet from spilled drinks and how no one cared but only went over to the bar for more.

"I'm going to dance with him," she said and just like that she was up to him and whispering something in his ear and they were dancing, the Yank dropping his crutches, his arms around her neck like she was the life ring and he was the sailor going down.

This time though it was a much bigger club and the Yank had more friends. Before long everyone had cleared away from the dance floor to watch them like they do in the cinema, this Yank being much more handsome and tall than the first and Angel looking even more pretty and fancied up than usual. She always danced with her eyes closed but just before the music stopped something must have made her open them. . . . She realized they were dancing alone. . . . She let go of him and pushed her way into the crowd like she was Cinderella caught out late with her prince.

"PardonmeI'vegottorun," and I met her at the door, the two of us running outside so fast we each gave the coat lady a shilling, giggling as madly as before.

Next day it was in the *Daily Mirror* how an American PFC named Michael Manning from Little Rock, Arkansas, had gone to a nightclub in Piccadilly with his buddies expecting just to watch on account of the wound he got in France when this beautiful young British gal came up to him out of the crowd near the bandstand and asked him to dance.

"Thanks doll, but I'm going to sit this one out," the paper said he said.

"Don't you think you could try?" the paper said the Yank said Angel said. "Try just for me?"

"Well, sure honey. If'n you hold me real tight that is."

And while his buddies stood there with their mouths open he really did dance, letting his crutches fall to the floor and dipping and bobbing with this British gal like it was old times back home and how the mysterious thing was just when he realized what had happened and people started yelling and applauding the girl disappeared, one moment she was there and the next she wasn't.

Angel's dad got the *Mirror* first thing every morning so we saw it soon enough. They had a picture of him standing in front of the bar with his crutches mounted crisscross over the Guinness sign like it was Lourdes. And the funny thing was we *still* didn't think much of it. Angel cut the picture out and carried it in her purse for a while but that's really all. We had new jobs in hospital kitchen, and I suppose we were too busy settling in to think much of anything.

It was only after the third, the bombardier without any knees, we started thinking maybe there was something to it. I remember she danced with some regular Yanks that night before spotting the one on crutches. All the papers had it on Sunday this time, most of them on the front page because there wasn't much happening in the war just then. That was when they started calling her "The Angel of Piccadilly" and all. I remember they went into more and more detail every time it happened. A tallish girl with a dimple on her left cheek they said, shoulder-length blonde hair about five feet nine with legs that would make a dead man climb straight out of his grave. They were right on the hair, wrong on the dimple, which she never had. But what was funny was it made it seem she was the escaped criminal and all, headlines saying "Where Will Angel Strike Next?" and so on. Made her seem the Ripper actually, the two of us reading the paper in the morning and not giggling anymore because neither of us was quite sure what was happening. But all along this great mystery of her disappearing was simply because we both had to get home and were afraid if we didn't her mum and dad would find out and we wouldn't be allowed our Saturday nights anymore.

I don't think she ever told anyone else it was her, Vee

134   Latchford, who was actually Angel, at least not during the war.
Afterwards she might have told Richard, but I'm not sure. I do
know they were all set to go down the aisle together and then
suddenly they weren't and I had to return a pretty chiffon dress
I'd bought special for the occasion. Richard hadn't been in the war
on account of his lungs—he was the jealous type and I suppose it
was too much for him thinking of her with all those Yanks and the
praying for her to come dance with them, like the papers said.

It's a wonder *we* remained friends come to that. A lot of pretty
girls are like Angel was, always wanting a less pretty one around
to act their witness. But I didn't mind actually. It got so I felt
protective over her being almost a year older than she was and
having lost a mum in the Blitz and so on.

"Well, what do you say to them?" I used to ask her at lunch
thinking that would be the important clue.

"I don't know," she said, spreading her chips around with her
fork to let them cool like she always did. "Mostly I tease them
is all."

"Tease them about what?"

"Why about not dancing, silly."

"They're on crutches, Vee!"

"I know. What about it?"

Angel never was what you would call a talker.

"Why is it always Yanks?" I asked her, deciding on a new tack
as it were.

"I feel so sorry for them really. Them being all alone over here
with no family or loved ones. I'll dance with a Tommy someday,
you see if I don't."

She really didn't know why it happened though and that was
the mystery of it and not her disappearing like the papers said.
Maybe it was her legs, I thought, thinking for her. They were
lovely long like the way we said those days, and the papers were
right about their being enough to make a dead man dance much

less a wounded one. Maybe it was the sweaters she wore. Maybe these men saw her you-know-whats looking so soft and round they couldn't resist the urge to put their arms around her, the rest happening naturally if you see. And if it wasn't her legs or her sweater, maybe it was her manner. Maybe, I used to tell her, they feel the pity you have for them and yet they don't feel ashamed of it, they feel it's somehow bigger than you are or they are or the war is. . . .

"I don't know actually," she said, chewing on gum her last Yank had given her when they were still in the teasing stage. "Listen, Kay. I have to decide right now. Are we going out Saturday night or aren't we?"

And what I think looking back really happened was that Angel was the right girl in the right place like Joan of Arc or somebody like that. Here she was this beautiful young girl who perfectly combined all the best qualities of her time and place, and here they were these handsome Yanks perfectly combining all the best qualities of their time and place and then London during the war and the raids and all the suffering and hoping was somehow mixed in too, and with all this, out of all this, a miracle—*seven* miracles—simply had to occur.

"I don't know really," she would say, mumbling now so I could barely hear her, "I only wish it would stop."

The truth was it got to be a burden for her being The Angel of Piccadilly and all. Dancing like that would have gone to a lot of girls' heads, and knowing her like I did I'd have bet it would have gone to hers, too, making her more the madcap and runaround than ever. But somehow it had just the opposite effect. She started biting her nails the fifth one—the more times it happened the less sure she felt about herself. For some reason it made her very sad, her growing to resent it like it was something keeping her from all the fun the other girls were having just then, the papers having stolen that fun away from her. She was afraid that she'd someday ask a soldier to dance and he wouldn't or what was even worse he would try to and collapse on the floor right there in front of her after letting go his crutches. I don't think she could have stood that you see. To protect herself she got so she made fun of the ones she had already danced with, saying well, his wound wasn't that bad, if it was bad he wouldn't have been there, only a cushy twisted ankle probably and anyone could have danced with him not just me.

But she bit her nails down to the quick just the same, and toward the end of 1944 we hardly went out on Saturday nights at all which was a shame because by then the blackout was over for good and V-E Day wasn't that far off. The only time I ever remembered her looking so sad and down in the dumps was the day I visited her in hospital after she broke her hip last year. I knew which room she was in, I knew when I walked in I would see her lying there, and still I couldn't bring myself to go in for the longest time.

There she was on the bed, her beautiful legs all wrapped in plaster and a pin in it besides which you couldn't see. But the shock of it was she'd already come down with pneumonia without her telling anyone, and they had put an oxygen mask over her face. I remember because the mask kept slipping off, and the matron became all superior and haughty when I went out and asked her to fix it, telling me to fix it myself if I was in such a hurry.

I sat there all afternoon on the edge of the bed. She could hear me, but she couldn't answer back which was probably fine with her, Angel being Angel. But the funny thing was her bed rested right against the window, and looking out toward the sky while she was sleeping I discovered for the first time what she meant by her Spitfire autumns. . . . That what she saw on the days she said it wasn't leaves or trees or anything like that but clouds in the sky, long and stringy ones reminding her of vapor trails the fighters would leave chasing bombers over the Thames back in the early days of the war when we were both girls. . . . How seeing clouds like that would bring it all back to her like nothing else could, the same way some people remember from the smell of burning wood or sugar. And we had a real Spitfire autumn in 1976, too. I remember all the clouds seemed to look like that, long narrow ones inward coiled on themselves like a necklace when you let it drop on the dresser, just as if there was a continuous dogfight going on high over London between ghost planes and ghost pilots right then and there.

After a bit I got up and left. I hired a private nurse to see to the oxygen and all, even though I couldn't really afford it, Jack never having believed in his dying much less life insurance. But I remember being angry because hospital was so crowded, beds out in the hall just like during the war, though they promised us that would all be over with once we won. What was worse were the looks on people's faces when you walked by, not like during the war when everybody had a smile no matter how bad off they were. People were angry, you could see that. Confused and angry and not sure who to blame for the fact they were lying there unattended in the halls of cold hospital and dying there for all anyone cared.

It was the same night this young cabinet minister came on the telly to tell us we had to tighten our belts again, that the time for miracles was at an end . . . that Englishmen should no longer expect miracles to happen. I mean it made it seem he was outlawing Angel and all she stood for really, shoving her off our history the same way the crowd had shoved her off the underground two weeks before. He sounded just like Mickey come to that. He even looked like him—each wavy hair pinned exactly in place, his eyes darting back and forth like they might miss some opportunity to score off someone if they stopped for even one second. A nation of Mickeys, that's what we're coming to if you were to ask me.

Sometimes I catch myself thinking well, Kay old girl, it would have been better if you had died in the Blitz after all, but then I feel ashamed of myself and remember the ones who really did die and I feel stronger and happier and more able to cope.

You still have to do what you can, you see. The Council held open house for pensioners Saturday nights, and I had started going a month or two before Angel's accident to help out with refreshments and all. It was quite fun actually—there were a lot of old soldiers and sailors about, and like I said before they weren't past asking, though to look at some of them you'd think they would be. I went every Saturday night. When Angel's studio closed that August and she had nowhere to go anymore, I invited her along thinking it would do her a world of good being among people like that, people who remembered the same times she did. At first she wouldn't because she was scared so of turning into one of those ladies who sit in Greenwich park staring off into the mist remembering and waiting to die. I told her it wasn't like that at all, but she still didn't want to go and wouldn't have gone either if Mickey hadn't forced her to.

It was like this you see. We'd been shopping one afternoon and I'd come into the flat with her afterwards, Angel having promised me Mickey wouldn't be there.

"Surprise!" he said, popping out the loo with his zipper half down. "Where have you lovely ladies been this fine autumnal afternoon?"

"Out being chased off the streets by the bloody foreigners," I said, there being no love lost like I mentioned.

"Times change," he said, rushing over to help Angel off with her coat. "You should get to know some of them like I do. In a business way that is. Fine people they are the Germans. A man's got to respect them for what they've done over there. The Arabs, too, for that matter. A man's got to adjust to the new order of things to get ahead in the world, now doesn't he?"

He always talked like that Mickey did. I was going to leave, but Sally came in and I had to stop for a decent bit, her being down with the flu. Mickey started talking about one of his "transfers" he was making that night, bragging how this Japanese businessman was taking him out to a fancy new club in Knightsbridge.

"It's called 'The War Room,'" he said, "Old propellers on the wall, all the birds wearing clothes from the forties. Really quite a kick actually. Only you can't get a pint there, leastways not by asking for it. All they serve is their house specials what they call Blood, Toil, Tears, or Sweat. You have to order one or the other."

"What's Blood?" Sally asked, making a face.

"Vodka and tomato. I prefer Sweat myself," and he laughed his little Mickey laugh. "How about coming with me tonight, Vee?"

That took me by surprise and I think it took Angel that way, too, judging by the way she spilled her tea. Sally wasn't fit yet and he needed what he called a "comely escort." You should have seen the way he looked at her asking, like it was the most important thing in the world only he didn't want to let it on. An eager cocker spaniel Mickey was, except for him being a snake.

"Well, you see I promised . . ."

"Promised who?" Mickey said, on her just like that.

"I promised Kay I'd go with her tonight."

You could see Mickey chewing his lip trying not to show how angry he was. He had to save face somehow, so when he heard where we were going he gave her some of his business cards.

"That's an idea," he said, like it was him suggested it in the first place. "If any of the old boys have war souvenirs laying about, you might have them ring me up."

That's the only way I got her to go, her being presented with two choices like that. And it's funny but she rather enjoyed herself that first night. I mean it wasn't a great mob of eighty-year-old soldiers standing about talking over old battles. Some of them had been hurt all right, and you could see it in their eyes more than anywhere else, but it was just a friendly time to chat and eat cake and maybe dance a little those that were feeling up to it.

That's where I first met John actually. He was a bit younger than some of them, having lied about his age to the recruiting sergeant when they were losing so many pilots they didn't care. He still looked like a boy if you forgot his legs and the bad times he'd been through, leaning there against the soda machine minding the record player and changing them when the time came. We got so we knew most of the regulars before long, Angel and I. We were regulars ourselves come to that. It was doing wonders for her I thought, and then one night after I finished drying the teacups who do I find in the hall with her raincoat on like she's about to leave but Angel, standing there all bent over and crying her eyes out.

I'd only seen her cry once before, that was the shock of it. And she was really crying, too, the way a grown woman cries when she's lost a husband or maybe a son. It was that kind of crying and another besides, the kind when a woman catches sight of herself in the mirror one day and knows it's gone, her looks, her figure, her being young and all. It was those two ways of crying combined.

"What's wrong, Vee?" I said, putting my arm around her and feeling near a cry myself, seeing her like that, makeup running down her face and her lips quivering the way they were.

"It's all so sad!"

That's the only thing she could manage. Just that over and over again between sobs.

"Why of course," I said. "Why of course it's sad, Vee. It's always sad come to that."

But I didn't have time to think much about it because that was the same night Angel broke her hip. She insisted she was better, so I let her go home alone, making her promise to ring me the second she got there. The tube was crowded, and her being already upset the pushing got her all in a panic and she started trying to fight her way to the next car where there was more room. But before she could make it the train stopped at Euston, and she was shoved out the door just like she was a sack of mail. But what was funny was her telling me how she had time to stop herself with her arms before hitting the wall, but how for some reason she had turned and taken the full of it with her hip instead. Angel doing that was like another person deliberately jumping on the rails.

I visited her all I could of course. But then she seemed to be getting better toward the end of October and wouldn't have me missing my Saturday nights out on her account, so that week I stopped at the Council house for a quick look-see on my way to hospital.

"Hello, stranger," John said, smiling like always, "Where's your girlfriend?"

I told him. He started shaking his head.

"Well, it's strange but do you know the last time you were here you were out in the kitchen when she comes up to me very quiet like and just stands there for a minute or two sizing me up as it were. I remember about ten it was because I'd just put on the Tommy Dorsey what I always save for last. She stands there in front of me just like you are now and all of a quick she comes right out and asks me to dance. Well, of course it was sweet of her, but I pointed to the sticks here and shook my head. She wouldn't take no for an answer though. She started sobbing like after a while. It was embarrassing don't you see, her sobbing that way and here I am in all this scrap iron."

"Oh, John!"

"What's wrong?"

"Pardon me, I've got to run," and just like that I was outside in the cold trying to get to the tube station before it closed. I made it all right—I remember sitting there squeezed in between these two

142   big Arabs and trying to keep my mind off things by looking at the
sign they had on the end of the car warning everyone not to waste
water on account of the past summer's drought. But that was over
with now, and the sign was all dog-eared so you could see underneath it to another sign warning everyone about unattended par-
cels lying about being terrorist bombs. This one was torn, too, and
back of it was a third just barely showing which was about saving
power during the winter of 1974 when the lights had gone off.
And the funny thing was I knew there was another poster under
that and another one under that and so on and so on . . . knew
you could peel all the layers back until you eventually got to old
yellow and purple ones warning what to do in a raid or warning
you about whispering to strangers. And that even this wasn't the
end of it and further back were signs warning about what to do in
the General Strike, what to do when the Zeppelins came.

But it was crowded like it must have been for Angel, and I never
did think I'd manage to change trains for hospital. It was so difficult just getting across the platform it made me think how it must
have been for my dad years ago trying to get across the burning
city to my mum. Only it was somehow worse for me because no
one else on the car spoke English. You could hear them jabbering
away in all these different languages but none of them English,
me sitting there with my eyes closed praying for Angel like all
those men did in the war, shutting my eyes tight and concentrating on her because she was the one thing the foreigners couldn't
take from me, the only thing I had left in all the noise and
pushing.

I remember thinking about us going to school together as girls
and the different masters we had. I remember thinking about
what a handsome couple she and Richard made and what a shame
it was they didn't go through with it. And then I had to change
trains again, and I suddenly started remembering the only other
time I'd ever seen Angel cry which was on V-E night thirty-some

years before . . . remembered how she'd been moping around the first few months of 1945 on account of the newspapers like I said and how it was our last chance to have some fun because we were young but not so young we didn't know that whatever happened after the war it would all be somehow different. Angel had made her mind up she would either prove herself that night or she wouldn't. Maybe all her Yanks had only been slightly wounded like she said. Maybe it was true they could have danced with anyone. So what we did that last night was go looking for the most crippled Yank we could find.

There were soldiers everywhere once we crossed the river, people dancing and singing and shouting. The clubs were packed tighter than we'd ever seen them before, but I remember it was sad and somehow lonely really, not happy like you might think seeing newsreels of it today, not as if the good times were just starting but as if they were all over with now and everyone wanted a last fling to remember them by.

I don't know how many pubs and nightclubs and canteens we stopped in. There were Yanks in all of them, some of them on crutches, too, but Angel wouldn't have any of it, saying well, he's just got a twisted ankle or a banged-up knee, tugging me out the door and in and about these dancing Tommys splashing about the fountains and climbing on the statues and all.

We ended up at Rainbow Corner in Piccadilly just like I knew we would, and there was her Yank, this tall, handsome lieutenant on crutches and God knows what else, a bandage full over one eye, a little scar underneath the other, looking fresh off the battlefield and it was a miracle he was even alive much less standing there.

"I'm going to dance with him."

"Don't Vee!"

She let go my arm and started patting her hair down so it fell over her forehead.

"Don't spoil it!" I said, pleading with her. "Please don't spoil it now. Not tonight!"

But of course there was no stopping her once she'd made up her mind. I was watching her very carefully, but then she disappeared in all the bouncing heads and it was only because it was midnight now and everyone was standing on the tables so no one minded me stepping up on the bar I found her at all. She had made it over to him all right—she was standing on tiptoe so she could whisper in his ear. I saw him frown and I saw her whisper some more without anything very much happening and I'm thinking well, it's too bad he won't or can't because she's never looked prettier and sweeter and more embraceable than she does tonight. These other Yanks were climbing up on the bar hugging and kissing me now so I had to break away only this time it was too late because I lost sight of her and I was just about to give up when I turned and looked the other way and saw two people all alone in the corner and it's Angel and her Yank swaying back and forth like they'd invented it, his crutches gone, Angel laughing and sobbing and holding onto him like she'd never let go. And *that* was Angel's miracle and not any of those others and later when we went outside into the crowds near the Palace I suppose we must have been the only two girls crying in London.

But anyway that's what I was thinking about last October on the long ride trying to get to Angel's bedside in time. And why I was sobbing to myself like that wasn't because of all the foreigners on the underground or me being afraid of not getting there. What I was afraid of was being the only one left to remember someday, the only one who could tell you how it was those days in the Blitz and then later on going about like that in Piccadilly. And I began thinking maybe that cabinet minister was right after all, that the time for miracles had passed and how that wasn't bad really because we still had them in our younger days. We still had miracles there in memory and what we could do now was have a quiet chat with each other about the old days, we could drink tea and not have to dance if we didn't want to, that the being with each other was somehow enough now. That's what I would have told her you see. I had it all planned out.

"And besides, Vee," I would have said. "It's not as if he was a Yank, now was it? It's not as if he was a bloody Yank!"

And Angel would have laughed at that and I would have kissed her and everything would have been all right.